RAPED

ON THE RAILWAY

http://www.birchgrovepress.com

ISBN:
978-0-9870956-8-8

Raped on the Railway was first published c. 1899 with the false imprint date 1894. It was issued, probably by Charles Carrington in Paris, on hand made paper in a limited edition of 300 copies with pictorial wrappers depicting a rape scene. The illustration is signed A. Lambrecht. Adolphe Lambrecht illustrated Carrington's translation of *The Mysteries of Verbena House: Les Mystères de la Maison de la Verveine*. A second edition of *Raped on the Railway* was issued c. 1904. It was also backdated to 1894 but printed on ordinary paper and printed in a limited edition of 500 copies. The author is unknown. Most of the poems, however, are lifted from Aleister Crowley's *White Stains*, which was published clandestinely, most probably by Leonard Smithers, in 1898. Verse excerpts are from Crowley's 'Rondels' [I], 'Mathilde,' 'Ode to Venus Callipyge,' and 'Ad Lydiam, Ut Secum A Marito Fugeret' [5]. This edition of *Raped on the Railway* is based on the 1904 reprint.

White Stains, The Mysteries of Verbena House, and *Les Mystères de la Maison de la Verveine* are available from Birchgrove Press.

Raped

on the

Railway

A TRUE STORY OF A LADY
WHO WAS FIRST RAVISHED AND THEN
CHASTISED ON THE SCOTCH EXPRESS

BIRCHGROVE PRESS
2011

THE LAW OF RAPE

THE LAW OF RAPE

WHAT EAVES-DROPPERS ARE IN DANGER OF SEEING, AND THE CONSEQUENCES THAT RESULT THEREFROM

I have always, as a doctor and a man of the world, had a horror of rape on infants and children. Nothing can be more shocking than to take a helpless child and endeavour to satisfy one's lust upon its innocent body. Cases of rape on vigorous adult women come under quite a different category. We all know of the clever answer which, it is said, was made by Catherine of Russia or, as other people say, Napoleon the First, to the woman who came with a complaint that she had been tripped on her back and ridden by some hot-blooded soldier against her will. The monarch took a sword and, drawing the blade from the scabbard, invited the violated woman to plunge the steel back again into the empty sheath while he wriggled it before her.

Of course the lady was unable to do so, and her case was consequently non-suited. Balzac has a similar delightful story where, instead of sword or scabbard, a piece of thread and the eye of a needle were employed, and instead of an Emperor, the person who posed the problem was a judge. But that is another story, as Rudyard Kipling would say, for the girl did succeed in a most ingenious manner, which proves how dangerous it would be if women were furnished as men are, and able to commit rapes on us.

For any of my readers who may be contemplating the luxury of rape on the servant-maid, or some beautiful cousin of the proper age, I think it only right to warn them not to get caught.

Probably there is no more delightful pleasure than getting the better of a much desired, stout-thighed, but unwilling, lady. But the devil of it is that if she be at all inclined to do so, she might make it what is elegantly termed: "damned hot" for her ravisher.

Those unfortunate gentlemen therefore who may be slow-witted enough to get nailed and collared in the fascinating act, will require to know the law on this subject. We take the liberty then to state that rape is defined in law to be "the carnal knowledge of a woman by force, and against her will." For a long period it was punished as a capital crime in this country, but penal servitude or imprisonment was substituted by the 24 and 25 Vict. c. 100, S. 48. Under this section it is enacted that — "whosoever shall be convicted of the crime of rape shall be guilty of felony, and being convicted thereof, shall be liable, at the discretion of the court, to be kept in penal servitude for life, or for any term not less than three years, or to be imprisoned for any term not exceeding two years, with or without hard labour. Since these changes have been made in the law, it has been alleged that the crime has undergone a considerable increase. Taylor, a great authority if there ever was one, on Medical Jurisprudence, says:

"Medical evidence is commonly required to support a charge of rape, but it is seldom more than corroborative, the facts are, in general, sufficiently apparent from the statement of the prosecutrix. There is, however, one case in which medical evidence is of some importance, — namely, when a false accusation is made. In some instances, as in respect to rape on infants and children, the charge may be founded on mistake, but in others there is little doubt that it is often willfully and designedly made, for motives into which it is here unnecessary to inquire. Amos remarked, that for one real rape tried on the Circuits in his time, there were on the average twelve pretended cases. In some few instances these false charges are at once set aside by medical evidence — in others, medical men may be sometimes the dupes of designing persons, but in the majority, the falsehood of the charge is proved by inconsistencies in the statement of the prosecutrix herself."

It is pleasant to know that some of these charges are made up, and that there is always a chance for a man to get off, although he may, after all, have really climbed between the lady's lovely legs. We give a newspaper extract, to illustrate our meaning.

DUDLEY WOMAN'S EXTRAOR-
DINARY STORY

AT the Dudley Police Court, seven powerfully built and intelligent looking men, all of about 20 years of age, were charged with feloniously assaulting Sarah Adams (40), Newhall Street, Dudley.

Mr S. defended.

Prosecutrix stated that she had lived apart from her husband for eleven months, but they had resumed cohabitation. On Saturday night, at about eleven o'clock, as she was walking from Tipton to Dudley, on the right-hand side of the road, she saw prisoners coming down on the opposite side, singing and shouting. She met them between the Guest Hospital and the goods station. The tallest of them left his companions, saying: "Good-night, kids," and crossing over to witness, placed his arm round her neck and observed: "You have got to come with us and dance us upon your belly." Witness said: "For God's safe let me go home." Her assailant however, replied: "Yes, when we've d.... d well rogered you," and dragged her across the road to his companions, who called out: "Bring her here." He then dragged her about 150 yards down the Tipton Road, to the turnstile from which the footpath goes to Fisher's Bridge. At the turnstile, the others laid hold of her, and she was violently pulled into the field, where she was thrown down behind the hedge adjoining the main road, her clothes thrown up over her head, and her drawers literally torn off. Witness, who had repeatedly called out while being dragged down the road, now pleaded for mercy, asking them if they had mothers and sisters. The reply was: "We would do the same to them if they were here." She continued to struggle, and one of them remarked: "If you don't shut up, we will shut you up for ever." Feeling faint, she said: "Let me have air; I think I am dying," but they paid no attention to her entreaties, and each, she alleged, criminally assaulted her. She also alleged that Smith put his hand into her pocket and took her purse. Hearing footsteps, she again called for help, and two men looked through a gap in the hedge and said: "It's a woman; let her go." Only one of her assailants was then molesting her, he being on the top of her body, and executing a series of violent movements, the others being engaged investigating the contents of her purse. The men who had come on the scene assisted her into the road, and conducted her as far as the railway station. Here they met a police officer, to whom she made a complaint, and to whom the two men who had befriended her gave their names. The men who had maltreated her followed them up the road, using foul and threatening language; but directly they saw the policeman they ran away.

Replying to Mr Ward, witness said she had been visiting a M^r and Mrs P. at Tipton, but refused to give their address. She admitted having been in more than one public-house in Tipton before she met her friends.

A man named Job Langford said he and a companion heard a commotion in a field near the Guest Hospital, and on looking through the hedge saw prosecutrix sitting, on the grass with a number of young men round her and her clothes tucked up in a most indecent way. She took his companion's arm, but neither in the field nor on the way to the railway station did she make any complaint of having been cohabited with against her consent.

The magistrates said no jury would convict on such evidence, and dismissed the charges.

It is not our intention here to go further into the law of this highly interesting subject. If any of our readers wish to do that, we would recommend them to read up the various textbooks, and particularly "Untrodden Fields of Anthropology," (Paris, 1898, 2 vols of 520 & 380 pages respectively). In this work he will find the whole subject handled in a most edifying manner, and, there is no doubt that he will become very interested.

Cases are given of a "White Woman violated by a Negro;" the "Trick of a Negro to get a White Woman;" and also, an "Account of the Little White Girl who was Deflowered by a Negro."

From the anthropological standpoint, there are cases of "Arab Criminal Assaults and Rapes;" "Rapes amongst Creoles and Negroes;" "Cases of Women who have Raped little Boys;" and other matters which we believe are not generally known.

For the erotic and eulogistic side of the subject, we can recommend the student to consult several, works described in "Bibliotheca Arcana," (1 vol. of 65 pages, Paris, 1898), where he will probably find all he may desire to know.

Now and again cases of rape on girls and women occur in railway trains.

Most people now living, who have passed life's meridian, will recall the famous case of Colonel Baker and the Fascinating, Finely-made, Talkative, Coaxing, Venturesome, Frightened, Inquisitive, Warm-blooded, Voluptuous, Cock-teasing, Young lady, whom, it is reported, he attempted to ravish. The gallant Colonel, no doubt liked, what is called, "a bit of skirt," or in other words, was, an ardent woman-hunter, and took his pleasure wherever he could find it. But many men, who knew Baker intimately, did not believe in his guilt. There are many girls, especially those of a fashionable, know-all kind, whom a little healthy slapping on their lovely, plump buttocks, would do infinite good; who delight in working a man up to a pitch of erotic paroxysm, and when he draws his sword to strike, shrink back in terror at the sight of the gleaming blade. Be all this as it may, we are happy to record that other cases have come before the Courts, where the woman was a willing, consenting, and most delighted victim.

But the two actors have nevertheless been held up before the Law to answer a charge of "public Immorality."

In a curious little pamphlet (1) printed on very thin paper, we remember to have read "a most scandalous case" which took place in a Railway carriage between a strongly-built Jesuit Priest, and a live, lovely, fornication-loving, pretty little Viscountess.

The persons implicated were the Rev. Father J. Dufour d'Astafford, boasting the vigorous age of 44 years, and living in the seaport-town of Brest, and Louise-Marie-Gabrielle Carpentier, widow of the Viscount of Valmont, who had arrived at the charming and tantalizing age of 22 years. This coition-loving little lady was described in the charge sheet as "small, of lively manner, displaying in her physiognomy a great freshness of colour and, besides her youth, a certain diabolical beauty". The worthy Jesuit was her spiritual director.

On the 9th of July 1872, on his return from Quimperlé, where he had been preaching, he met Mme de Valmont at Châteaulin, where they took the train together for Brest. Familiarities in their conduct being observed at the station, the guard of the train, Kergroen, was directed by the station-master to keep

---

(1) Following is the title: *Tribunal correctionnel de Brest.* — Une extravagance judicaire. *Procès du R. P. Dufour & Madame la Vicomtesse de Valmont.* — I° Réquisitoire; — 2° Interrogatoire; — 3° Plaidoires; — 4° Jugement; — 5° Appréciations. Reproduction interdite.

an eye upon them. This he did; and passing along the train whilst it was in motion, he surprised them in the following equivocal positions. I quote Kergroen's deposition.

"I recognised the priest; he was on the left in a corner and the lady was in front of him, in the opposite corner. The lady had taken off her hat, the shade had been drawn over the lamp. The priest had his legs stretched out on the seat in front of the lady. When, later, I passed again before the carriage, the positions were changed, the lady holding the priest round the neck and kissing him. The priest no longer had his legs stretched out, the lady was seated on his knees, and was kissing him continually, whilst he was holding her round the waist."

"It seemed to me that it was time to interfere, and, I therefore entered the carriage, and told them they should not behave like that on the railway. The lady turned quite pale, but the priest replied: "We beg to offer you our excuses, we certainly are like children; after all, it is quite permissible for a brother and sister to kiss each other."

"Yes," I answered, "but even between brother and sister it is hardly correct to kiss each other like that."

Kergroen demanded the priest's card, which was refused, so he laid the matter before the station-masters of the two next stations at which the train stopped. This apparently plain statement of the case did not satisfy the president; he required more details, and the following dialogue took place:

The Judge: "You said at Quimerch and Landerneau that the lady was seated upon the knees of the priest. Before the examining magistrate, you made this statement far more grave by modifying it. You assert that she was seated astride, that is to say with her legs wide apart, and in a most improper position. These variations are of importance, with regard to the category of the offence, because in your statement you declared that you had witnessed an act of public immorality."

The Witness: "Yes, and I maintain, that in my view there really was an act of public indecency, if a woman is seated on a clergyman's knees, and when I was obliged to warn them by tapping the naked thighs of the lady."

The Judge: "Such an act on your part was very reprehensible, and in itself an offence against modesty. It would have been sufficient to warn them by the voice alone, and your voice is loud enough to do that."

The Witness: "I beg your pardon, the train was in motion and the evidence of the fact was more than complete when I was thus able to verify the lady's nakedness."

In answer to questions put to him by the station-master of Landerneau and others, the Rev. Father Dufour replied in a strain worthy of his order.

After having given his name, this gentleman stated that he had not persisted in affirming that his travelling-companion was his sister; he had simply said that he had known her for a long time, that she had rendered him certain services and that, out of gratitude, he had kissed her.

"*Where is the evil?*" added the priest, "*If we had been brother and sister, we could have done so. Suppose,*" said he again to the Police-Inspector, "*two young married people who are travelling by rail, can they not kiss each other and even do something else? We had not done any evil. Every day people newly married allow themselves certain liberties while they are travelling; where is the wrong?*"

At his trial Father Dufour excused himself in the following unmanly, hypocritical manner:

"If I have once on the railway drawn the curtain over the lamp, — which I do not believe I did, — it would be only because I am a great sleeper when travelling on the line.

"I was wrong to stretch myself out upon the seat, although in travelling, one is permitted to enjoy this license. Madame de Valmont, seated at first at the other end of the compartment, drew nearer to me, because the noise of the train prevented us from hearing each other. She thanked me for having stopped for her at Chateaulin; and in the expression of her gratitude, *she approached her head near to my breast to such an extent, that her face may have touched my chin.*"

The case was tried on the 4th and judgment given on September 10th 1872. The Judge, a liberal broad-minded Man of the World, evidently considered that, law or no law, a dainty lady with burning thighs, and separated momentarily from her husband, might very well be allowed to give refuge to the flaming priapus of a vigorous celibate priest. It must also be born in mind that the Messalinie tendencies of many a high-born voluptuous lady are satisfied by the kind priests, who think that while working for God, they may also do a little on their own account.

Again, many a lady of high society is wedded to an old and impotent husband who is not able to do more than tickle and tease, or rub and poke them about, until they succeed in rousing the woman's passionate Nature to an extent they are themselves unable to cope with it. In such cases, if the lady does not take the footman or a strong-backed coachman or some lecherous friend of her husband, she has recourse to her spiritual adviser. Think of the consequences, if this lady were to take some man in the street. She would be liable to catch some hideous disease or, apart from that, be subject perhaps to blackmail by her Paramour, whose honesty might prove to be less strong than his tool.

We are happy to record that the Priest and the Viscountess were acquitted, and we can only hope that this skirt-loving priest, threw his to the winds, and married the charming little lady whose white thighs had been made a public spectacle for the sake of his love.

Other men, before now, have honourably espoused women they have been the cause of bringing into public shame. Some scoundrels, we know, have deserted the sweetheart whom they had gotten with child, or abandoned the woman who has been divorced for having yielded herself to her lover's lust. But this does not prove they were right. Of course, we do not say that a man is bound to marry every woman he gets down upon her back, but there are cases where he is obliged and in duty bound to do so. The following instance, recorded by some unknown Byron, illustrates our point:

THE VIOLATED NYMPH. (2)

The four and twentieth day of May,
Of all days in the year,
A virgin Lady fresh and gay,
Did privately appear;
Hard by a River side got she,
And did sing loud the rather,
'Cause she was sure, she was secure,
And had intent to bathe her.

With glittering, glancing, jealous Eyes,
She slyly looks about,
To see if any lurking spies
Were hid to find her out:

And being well resolved that none,
Could see her Nakedness,
She pulled her robes off one by one,
And did her self undress.

---

(2) The date of this charming little poem is about 1707.

Her purple Mantle fring'd with Gold,
Her Ivory Hands unpin;
It would have made a
Coward bold,
Or tempted a Saint to sin.

She turn'd about and look'd around
Quoth she, I hope I'm safe,
Then her rosie Petticoat,
She presently put off.

The snow white Smock which she had on,
Transparently to deck her,
Look'd like Cambric or Lawn,
Upon an Alabaster Picture:
Thro' which Array I did faintly spy.
Her Belly and her Back,
Her Limbs were straight, and all was white,
But that which should be black.
Into a flowing Stream she leapt,
She looked like *Venus'* Glass.
The Fishes from all quarters crept,
To see what Angel 'twas.
She did so like a Vision look,
Or Fancy in a Dream.
'Twas thought the Sun the Skies forsook,
And dropt into the Stream,
Each Fish did wish himself a Man,
About her all was drawn,
And at the Sight of her began
To spread abroad their Spawn:
She turn'd to swim upon her Back,
And so displayed her Banner,
If Jove had then in Heaven been,
He would have dropt upon her.
A Lad that long her Love had been,
And could obtain no Grace,
For alt her prying lay, unseen,
Hid in a secret place:
Who had often been repuls'd
When he did come to Woo her,

Pull'd off his Cloaths, and furiously
Did run and leap into her.

She squeak'd, she cry'd, and down she div'd,
He brought her up again,
He brought her o'er upon the Shore,
And then and then and then.
As *Adam* did Old *Eve* enjoy,
You may guess what I mean,
Because she all uncover'd lay,
He cover'd her again.
With watery Eyes she pants and cries
« I'm utterly undone,
If you will not be wed to me,
E'er the next Morning Sun. »
He answer'd her he ne'er would stir,
Out of her Sight till then,
« We'll both clap Hands in Wedlock Bands
Marry, and to't again. »

Little did I think, whilst reading this account, that I should one day be asked by a friendly and enterprising publisher to write down some of my recollections on the subject of rape, which, I may as well mention, has always been a favourite subject with me. If I detest violence to children, I adore a victory won over a woman. To get a strong-bodied wench, in the prime of health, down on her back, and triumph over her virtue, in spite of all her struggles, is to my mind the height of delightful existence, the sum of all human ambition. Rapes on children seem to me unnatural, and like eating fruit before it is mature. The same considerations can hardly apply to a ripe, full-grown, perfectly developed woman. To her, the friction, contact, and embraces of man, flesh to flesh close-locked and intertwined, is as much a necessity as eating and drinking, and sleeping and breathing. Many women cannot be made to appreciate this philosophy until they have been violently taken against their will, and made to taste of that fruit for which they afterwards entertain such a passionate liking.

The account here set forth may be taken as strictly exact. In "nothing I have extenuated," I can truly add that "naught have I set down in malice." All the events narrated in the following pages occurred to a friend still living, and who is ready to step forward in attestation of their veracity. I write only from the vantage-ground of a disinterested person, a sort of invisible witness, faithfully recording all details, without over-stepping the bounds of moderation.

EUSTON STATION

EUSTON STATION

THE entrance to Euston Station is of itself sufficiently imposing. It is a high portico of brown stone, old and grim, in form a casual imitation, no doubt, of the front of the temple of Nike Apteros, with a recollection of the Egyptians proclaimed at the flanks. The frieze, where of old would prance an exuberant procession of gods, is, in this case, bare of decoration, but upon the epistle is written in simple, stern letters the word, "EUSTON." The legend, reared high by the gloomy Pelagic columns, stares down a wide avenue. In short, this entrance to a railway station does not in any way resemble the entrance to a railway station. It is more the front of some venerable bank. But it has another dignity, which is not born of form. To a great degree it is to the English, and to those who are in England, the gate to Scotland.

The platform at Euston, a few minutes before the Scotch Express starts, is one of those sights which will provide a philosopher with food for thought, whatever may be the bent of his mind. Apart from the passengers, concerning each of whom it is possible to mentally construct a little tragedy or comedy, there is the huge red engine throbbing with suppressed strength until the moment when it is permitted to bound forward with its living freight of passengers with all their cares, pleasures, griefs, joys, businesses, or errands of mercy or mischief.

By the side of the metal monster, stood a quiet-looking man in grey, who was to direct and control it on its course. The fireman was pouring oil from a long-necked can into various brass-cups, and the guard, resplendent in a uniform ornamented with silver braid, strutted up and down the platform, touching his cap now and again, with a deference born of many tips, to some quiet-looking middle-aged gentleman who was doubtless some nobleman on his way to visit his Scotch estates.

It wanted but ten minutes to starting time, and most of the passengers had already ensconced themselves comfortably in their seats. The only exceptions were those who were being "seen off" by relatives or friends; some of these passengers were old travellers who had taken the precaution to secure their seats before exchanging the last words and farewell kisses with their wives or other female relatives.

Others, on the contrary, had not troubled to secure seats, being well aware that it is only on rare occasions, such as the beginning of the grouse-shooting or salmon-fishing season, that the Scotch Express is ever crowded.

Amongst these last was a young man dressed in a tweed suit, and wearing a travelling cap. His face was handsome, though rather impudent-looking, and there was a half observant, half-merry twinkle in his blue eyes. A long fair moustache partially concealed a firm-looking, clear cut mouth. His auburn hair curled closely over a well-shaped head. It was difficult to tell from his appearance what was his profession, and you might easily have guessed him to be a soldier, or an artist, or a literary man, or perhaps a young gentleman of no profession at all.

He sauntered up and down the platform, arm in arm with a friend who was of quite a different type. He was attired in a black frock coat, and wore the regulation black stove-pipe hat, and from his clean shaven chin and mutton chop whiskers it was easy to guess that he belonged to one of the "discreet" professions, and was either a doctor or a lawyer. The latter surmise would have been the correct one, for Henry Lawrence was a barrister, and though he had not long been called to the bar he was already on the way to secure a large practice.

His friend, whom we first described, was named Robert Brandon, and was an artist. The two had been school-fellows and college chums, but after they left Oxford, their roads in life had separated, and for the next few years they saw little or nothing of each other, but a few months previously Brandon had returned to London, and one of his first acts had been to find out his old friend, and renew their acquaintance. A real affection had sprung up between the two men, who were both of the same age, and had many tastes in common — amongst them being a partiality for "a bit of skirt."

In the beginning of the spring, Robert Brandon had gone over to the Continent on a sketching tour, and after being absent for three or four months, had returned to London; but a few days after his arrival, an important letter had summoned him to the North, and he was about to start by the Scotch Express.

As the two young men sauntered up and down the platform, the following conversation took place between them.

"Sooner or later I'll serve you out for the trick you play me," said Henry Lawrence.

"I must tell you for the tenth time, my dear Henry, that I am absolutely forced to return home. I am expected, in order to treat of important business!

"Hum! no doubt, some petticoat business!"

"No, I assure you..."

"Oh! I know you well, you joker," answered the lawyer, smiling. "You are a dreadful rake, and at the same time the greatest skeptic in love that it is possible to come across. The fair Swiss maidens have been cruel to you, and you are impatient to seek compensation for their harshness; that's why you can give me only half a day."

"Quite a mistake, old chap, and, if I had only felt so inclined, I could have reaped an ample harvest of hearts and virgin ones, or nearly so, in the midst of the glaciers."

"In the camp of hotel chambermaids?"

"Naturally so, Switzerland is at present deficient in native or naturalized princesses for the use of tourists."

Lawrence smiled and passed his tongue sensually over his lips.

"I catch you in the very act," continued Brandon, "and I tremble at the thought of the hecatomb of maidenheads you must have taken among the native girls... But the train will start in five minutes and I must first find a seat, so I have only just time to shake hands once more..."

"What already," said Lawrence shaking his head, "when shall I see you again?"

"Whenever you like to come and stay with me for a couple of months."

"You are out of your senses, my poor Brandon."

"I've been so often told so that I begin to believe it almost."

At that moment one of the officials shouted in stentorian tones, "Any more passengers for the North? Take your seats please," and after shaking hands warmly with his friend, Brandon directed his steps towards the train.

Wishing to find a snug corner, in which to pass the night comfortably, Brandon, his travelling rug on his arm, walked rapidly down the train and looked inside the carriages, and found all those at the head of the train chock full.

Brandon, in rather a bad humour, was about to jump into the very first carriage, when he stopped all at once before an empty compartment.

Not quite empty though. There was at the extreme end in the far corner, with her back to the engine, a lady, wrapped up in furs and travelling wraps, and whose face was completely hidden behind a thick veil. All that could be distinguished were two large brilliant eyes, shining from behind the veil like two diamonds set in ivory.

The train was at this time engineless, but presently a railway "flier," painted a glowing vermilion, slid modestly down and took its place at the head. The guard walked along the platform, and decisively closed each door. He wore a dark blue uniform, thoroughly decorated with silver braid in the guise of leaves. The way of him gave to this business the importance of a ceremony. Meanwhile the fireman had climbed down from the cab and raised his hand, ready to transfer a signal to the driver, who stood looking at his watch. In the interval there had something progressed in the large signal-box that stands guard at Euston. This high house contains many levers, standing in ranks. It perfectly resembles an organ in some great church, if it were not that these rows of numbered and indexed handles typify something more acutely human than does a keyboard. It requires four men to play this organ-like thing, and the strains never cease. Night and day, day and night, these four men are walking to and fro, from this lever to that lever, and under their hands the great machine raises its endless hymn of a world at work, the fall and rise of signals and the clicking swing of switches.

And so, as the vermilion engine stood waiting and looking from the shadow of the curve-roofed station, a man in the signal-house had played the notes which informed the engine of its freedom. The driver saw the fall of those proper semaphores which gave him liberty to speak to his steel friend. A certain combination in the economy, of the London and North Western Railway, a combination which had spread from the men who swept out the carriages through innumerable minds to the general-manager himself, had resulted in the law that the vermilion engine, with its long string of white and bottle-green coaches, was to start forthwith toward Scotland.

Presently the fireman, standing with his face toward the rear, let fall his hand. "All right," he said. The driver turned a wheel, and, as the fireman slipped back, the train moved along the platform at the pace of a mouse. To those in the tranquil carriages this starting was probably as easy as the sliding of one's hand over a greased surface, but in the engine there was more to it. The monster roared suddenly and loudly, and sprang forward impetuously. A wrong-headed or maddened draft-horse will plunge in its collar sometimes when going up a hill. But this load of burdened carriages followed imperturbably at the gait of turtles. They were not to be stirred from their way of dignified exit by the impatient engine. The crowd of porters and transient people stood respectfully. They looked with the indefinite wonder of the railway-station sightseer upon their faces at the windows of the passing coaches. This train was off for Scotland. It had started from the home of one accent to the home of another accent. It was going from manner to manner, from habit to habit, and in the minds of these London spectators there surely floated dim images of the traditional kilts, the burring speech, the grouse, the canniness, the oatmeal — all the elements of a romantic Scotland.

SIXTY MILES AN HOUR

WHAT TOOK PLACE
IN A FIRST-CLASS CARRIAGE
OF THE SCOTCH EXPRESS

THE painter felt a slight tremor run through his limbs, then, with a toss of his head, he jumped into the compartment in which the lady was seated, saying to himself:

"Humph! it smells of *odor femina* here..." Brandon cast another glance at the lady and noticed that her appearance was quite distinguished, and that her apparel denoted elegance and good taste.

Employing then a simple ruse, but which is nearly always successful, the artist closed the door and put his head out of the window, so as to deter any other travellers from coming into his compartment.

His heart was beating with force, and he was not quite reassured until he heard the signal given to start.

When the train began slowly to leave the station, the painter left the window and turned towards the lady, who was seated in the opposite corner of the carriage.

He noticed, with some vexation, that instead of looking towards him, she had half turned round and was looking out of the window on her side at the network of lines, and was apparently taking a great interest in the men who were shunting the carriages.

At all events the London North Western Railway is not like some other lines, and does not keep the passengers in semi-darkness. The lamps give a fairly bright light, and enable travellers to see one another, and even tolerably well. Brandon was therefore able to take stock of the lady, and make up his mind as to what her social condition was.

He noticed that she was rather a little woman, but exceedingly well-made, as he was able to see, for she had not put on any shawls or wraps — the weather indeed being too warm to render them necessary — and she wore a tightly fitting tailor-made costume which showed off her figure to perfection. She had crossed one leg over the other, and thus displayed a neat foot and a pretty ankle, the latter encased in openwork, black, silk stockings. On her head was a coquettish grey felt hat, and fastened round it was a large white veil, which completely covered, though it did not conceal altogether, the lady's features.

Brandon was able to notice her face tolerably well, and saw that she had a very pretty mouth, though he judged from the lips that they were not only eminently kissable, but would return a kiss with interest, or indeed, he thought, give even a warmer proof of affection if their owner wished it and was enamoured of a man. The rather wide nostrils of the delicately tip-tilted nose seemed to confirm this theory. The hair was wavy, and of that rich chestnut brown which always grows in profusion and not only on the head, as Brandon was well aware, for he had seen many nude models in the course of his artistic career. The eyes, which, as we have said, were very bright, had long eyelashes which served to intensify the sudden glances which were shot from behind them. On the whole Brandon came to the conclusion that he had seldom seen a prettier little woman.

"To what class of society does this woman belong?" thought the painter, vexed at not attracting her attention. "She is rich, undoubtedly, and her exterior as far as I can judge, denotes a woman of the world... but of which world? Is she a great lady? No, she would not travel alone... A rich *bourgeoise?* It may be, but I doubt it, for she has in her manners a certain air of distinction and independence which is almost exclusively the appendage of artistes... Yes, she must be an artiste... or else perhaps a kept-woman..."

Before Brandon could make up his mind on these points the train had glided rapidly through the suburbs of London, and having once shaken off « villadom » was speeding along at a rate which would not cease increasing till it exceeded sixty miles an hour, towards Crewe, the first stopping-place on this long journey.

The painter was not one of those enterprising Don Juans who cannot find themselves in tête-à-tête with a woman without feeling an imperative desire to effect her conquest, but he was fond of adventure, of the mysterious and unexpected everything that makes a great impression on the imagination.

If, instead of hiding her features beneath an almost impenetrable veil, the lady with whom he found himself had allowed him to see her face, it is probable that he would have limited himself to the exchange of a few polite words with her without seeking to push his gallantry any further.

But the indifference with which she seemed to regard him piqued his pride, and he determined to oblige her to take notice of him.

Like most artists, Brandon sometimes neglected parliamentary forms, and spoke out with a degree of familiarity rather unusual in aristocratic drawing-rooms.

Determined to force his travelling companion to answer him, he got up, and going right up to her, he took off his cap, and bowing low, said to her:

"Will you be good enough, Madam, not to be offended at the request I am about to make to you?..."

The lady, who had turned briskly round when the painter advanced towards her, looked him in the face, and answered rather haughtily:

"I have not authorized you to speak to me, Sir."

"That is true, and I humbly confess my fault."

"Well, what is it you wish?"

"Pray excuse the boldness of an artist, who has the misfortune much oftener to frequent studios than drawing-rooms."

"Ah! you are an artist?" said the lady in an almost amiable tone.

"Yes, Madam; Brandon, a painter no doubt unworthy to reproduce the divine features which you so obstinately persist in hiding beneath that ugly lace armour;" replied the painter, boldly, taking his seat in front of the lady.

"Your name is known to me, Sir, and better still, some of your works of art," said the lady, inclining her head graciously, "and I think you calumniate yourself when you make yourself so humble."

While the lady was speaking, the artist could notice the brilliant white of her neck, the opulent charms of her breast, the admirable contour of her chin, in which a voluptuous dimple nestled, and the seductive tone of her voice.

Nothing more was required to set fire to him, as is vulgarly said.

"Pray, Madam, do not treat me with so much indulgence," he rejoined; "you would be authorizing me to give expression to my gratitude, and then..."

"Oh! then, you might be wanting in respect to me?"

"Oh! Madam..."

"Let us come back to your request. What was it you were about to ask me?"

"Pardon me, I pray you; the emotion you cause me is so great that I have quite forgotten what I wanted."

"It was therefore but of very slight importance... If you can see no objection, Sir, I will try to go to sleep, for I feel tired; good night..."

The lady took up a cloak which was lying on the seat beside her, and throwing it round her so as to cover all the lower part of her face, she rested her head against one of the divisions which separate the seats, and closed her eyes.

Brandon bit his lips till they bled.

This sudden end of an adventure which had begun by giving him smiling hopes, wounded his vanity to the quick, and far from giving up the game, he determined to stake his all.

During about twenty minutes, the painter tried to renew hostilities with some serious chances of success.

The lady slept or appeared to sleep.

Her breathing was slow and regular, and from her whole person there emanated a fragrant odour of violets, which completed the intoxication of the artist.

He had suddenly fallen in love, he could not have said with whom. This woman, whom he supposed to be pretty because she was richly and elegantly dressed, had just made a claim upon his chivalrous sentiments, by falling asleep near to him without showing the slightest fear, and he dared not abuse her confidence.

And yet, it was not good-will that was wanting in him.

"Ah bah!" said he to himself, "I should be a great fool to go on acting like a timid school-boy. I am certain that the lady would not fail to laugh at me to-morrow morning."

After having vainly troubled his brains to find a means of galvanizing the lovely sleeper, Brandon ended by employing the vulgar dodge, familiar to libertines who are getting old, and to unmannerly rakes and to timid lovers.

He slowly approached his foot to the lady's boot and gently touched it...

The lady did not budge.

Brandon pushed a little harder, he had even the audacity to slightly caress the tip of the foot of the fair sleeper. It seemed as if she had suddenly become petrified, for she made no movement to avoid the attack of her fellow-traveller.

Little by little the painter had become excited; his brain was on fire, his heart was throbbing, and he was shaken by furious desire...

He could no longer be mistaken, the lady was encouraging him by not resisting his amorous enterprises.

Carrying audacity to its utmost limits, Brandon tenderly pressed between his two feet the delicate ankle of the lady. He was about to lean forward towards her to take her hand, when she suddenly lifted her head, and said to him in a bantering tone:

"I should much like to know, Sir, why you persist in crushing my toes?"

The painter was for a moment silent, then taking courage, he replied:

"Because this is the most eloquent means I can employ to make known my sentiments to a pretty woman who pretends to be asleep."

"And what sentiments, pray! can I inspire you with? You have never seen me."

"My heart does not require the aid of my eyes to guess that you are as charming as witty."

"Granted; I am charming and possess much wit; what do you conclude therefrom?"

"Oh! Madam!" said Brandon, all on fire at once, "I do not believe, ever to have experienced in all my life, such exquisite sensations... You are an enchantress."

At the same time he seized the hand of the fair unknown and imprinted on her wrist several ardent kisses...

The artist felt an unspeakable joy in noting the slight start she made, anticipating that she was about to give way to him...

But suddenly, releasing her arm by a sharp movement, the lady said to him in a severe tone:

"Cease, Sir, I command you. I wanted to see how far your audacity would venture. I know now. I consent to forgive your insulting enterprises, but on one condition; that you go back to the corner you at first occupied when you entered his carriage."

"No!" replied Brandon, forcibly, for he was so excited that he was no longer master of himself. "I feel myself attracted to you so irresistibly, that I will hesitate before no consideration, before no danger to make you accept my homage..."

"Is it possible... such language to me?..."

"It is that of a man madly in love... we are alone... no one will ever know what has taken place here, it is a minute of divine intoxication that we steal from heaven and the voluptuous remembrance of which will be the delight of our life... Give way to my prayers, I conjure you! Do not transform these instants of happiness into a barbarous struggle... Love me as I love you."... Brandon had rushed towards the lady, he again seized her hand, and suddenly pulling aside her cloak, he implanted two burning kisses on her neck...

"Sir, Sir, I implore you..." murmured the fair traveller in a dying voice, the precursor of her defeat. "It is abominable of you to thus take advantage of my situation..."

"I love you! I love you!" cried the artist in the acme of excitement as he furiously pressed the unknown in his arms.

He would probably have triumphed over her last resistance when the speed of the train was suddenly slackened.

At once the railway porters ran along the platforms, shouting:

"Crewe! Crewe! Stop here ten minutes..."

The doors flew open and most of the travellers hastened to get out.

Nothing can give an idea of the consternation depicted on Brandon's face at finding his amorous enterprises interrupted by the stoppage of the train. In a few seconds, ten different fears had crossed his mind.

The lady, having recovered her presence of mind, might henceforth keep him at a distance, claim the protection of the railway officials or change her carriage.

Other travellers might enter their compartment...

It was in fact this which was very nearly taking place.

A stout man, his head buried in a fur cap, and with his rug on his arm, got on to the step and was about to enter the compartment occupied by the artist. The latter, his face purple and his eyes glaring, stood suddenly before the intruder.

"Where are you going?" said he angrily.

"Why here!" said the traveller, astonished.

"There's no room."

"I beg your pardon, I see only you and a lady in this compartment.

"I repeat to you, all the places are taken," rejoined the painter boldly... "A family of six persons has just got down... Here they are, coming back..."

Brandon pointed at the same time to a family who were hastening up.

The stout gentleman made a gesture of annoyance, and hurried away grumbling.

The painter gave a sigh of relief, as he quickly closed the door, behind which he kept until the train had started again.

Delivered from his fears, Brandon hastened back to the side of the lady.

"Ah! Madam!" said he, putting his hand to his heart, "what anguish I have just gone through!"

"How so?" asked the lady, artfully.

"This man who was on the point of interposing himself between us... I saw the moment when it would have been necessary to renounce...!"

"Renounce what?" said the fair traveller.

"The happiness of embracing you, life of my soul..."

The artist sat down next to the lady, and, passing his arm round her waist, said to her:

"I implore of you, my angel, to let me contemplate those heavenly features I so burn to portray."

"Do not count upon that, Sir."

"But why? Oh! why?"

The fair traveller again disengaged herself, and turning upon Brandon eyes which glistened like burning coals beneath her veil, she said to him in a hesitating tone:

"Promise me not to seek to see my features, and I may perhaps be weak enough to give way to your entreaties..."

"Are you then married?"

"What can it concern you? You will never meet me again, and the memory of me will soon be effaced from your mind like a dream..."

Brandon, in the paroxysm of desire, promised all the lady demanded.

"When we get to Glasgow," she said to Brandon, "we shall separate, never more to see each other; such is my will; do not make me repent of my weakness..."

"I love you! I love you to distraction!" exclaimed the artist with vehemence, "and now that you have half opened to me the gates of Heaven, you must be mine for ever! Come, adorable mistress, no longer hide from me thy divine features, for surely art thou a celestial creature..."

At the same moment the painter seized hold of the corner of the veil hiding the features of the fair traveller, which he lifted up to the height of her forehead; but she promptly stood up and pulled it down again with such rapidity, that he had barely time to catch the ensemble of her features...

He was however able to recognize that this woman was a thousand times more lovely than he had supposed, and he had time to remark on her temple, a beauty spot of the size of a pea...

Irritated at the resistance of the fair unknown, and blinded by passion, the artist again advanced towards her to lift up her veil.

"Beware!" said the lady, pointing at him the muzzle of a little ivory-handled revolver; "if you advance but one step forward, you are a dead man."

"To die by thy hand at this moment, is to seal my felicity," replied Brandon, decided to brave the danger in order to satisfy his ardent wishes... Was it written that he should NOT see the features of his mistress of one night?...

At the moment that he stretched forth his hand to seize her, she put her finger to the trigger of her revolver... The pistol did not go off, for there was a loud screech from the engine, and the powerful Westinghouse brakes brought the train to such a sudden standstill that the shock would have caused the lady to fall, if Brandon had not caught her in his arms.

THE PAINTER'S WIFE

THE PAINTER'S WIFE

WE will here leave the painter in the train, while we give a short description of the man, and some account of his antecedents.

Strong, square-shouldered, and with that well set-up appearance which is acquired by drill, he looked every inch what he had really been, a Captain in a crack cavalry Regiment. He had seen some fighting in his time, as the sword-cuts on his chest and legs, had he cared to show them, would have proved. He came of a fighting family. His brother had fallen in a charge, and his father owed the whiteness of his head less to the cares of age than to the anxiety of a forlorn hope that he had once led.

Our hero had quitted the Regiment partly for love of a woman, and partly owing to a duel with a French officer, in which he had maimed his man for the rest of his days. Owing to the scandal created by this affair, and a few tales circulated by slanderous tongues concerning a little supposed cleverness with the cards, Brandon had resolved to resign his commission and live on the ample fortune he had at his command.

In the first years of his freedom, he wandered about the world with his handsome wife, and found his way into all manner of strange places.

Clever and cute as he was, he at last met his masters and fell into the hands of a gang of sharpers who flitted between Ostend and Monaco. Like all people who lose money in these places, he at first had a run of luck, winning large sums. Elated by success, he continued playing, only to find the tables turning against him. He then, of course, commenced to plunge, and losing his habitual caution, grew perfectly reckless. After ten days hard play he left the gorgeous gaming Palace a ruined man, white, haggard, and broken-down. His ten day's play had aged him five years. After spending the remainder of his fortune, he took to painting, for which he had always had a strong predilection; indeed, he was no mean amateur.

It was about this time that he commenced to notice a change in the bearing of his wife towards him. She was still beautiful beyond compare, and while the change of fortune had only increased his love for her, it had weakened hers for him.

She was only thirty years of age and splendidly built, and her small waist and magnificent breasts were the cynosure of all eyes. She was plump, fresh coloured, and had large greyish eyes, swimming in an ocean of voluptuousness, with red, slightly sensual lips. She would have made a capital banquet for a king. In fact, we are inclined to believe that had King David seen her, he would have overlooked the seduction of Bathsheba for the pleasure of dwelling between the thighs of Brandon's wife. It required, too, a King's purse to satisfy all the whims and caprices of this lady for dress. In the days of their wealth, toilet had formed one of the heaviest items in their expenditure. And now that they had fallen upon evil days, she could not forego the fine feathers that had once been the delight of her heart. Instead of endeavouring to humour his wife, Brandon tried to frown down this weakness.

The inevitable result was that his wife resorted to adultery in order to procure those articles of dress that she coveted. She paid for them as the vulgar saying goes, upon her back, with wriggling buttocks and legs in the air.

At last the painter had no further doubt. The tales

he had heard, and had wished not to believe, could no longer be ignored: his wife had a lover. The strangest thing about it was that he should have so long remained in ignorance as to the fact. He must have known well that the low prices which were paid for his pictures were hardly sufficient for the needs of the household, let alone the terrible prices marked on the invoices that were sent home with the goods she had purchased.

She often went out driving in Hyde Park, and on long lonely country-roads, in the fashionable carriage of the Count de Sainte-Galette, a French nobleman who had been setting London society by the ears for the last two years, on account of his extravagance. When she came home in the evening after the theatre very late, her hair looked as though she had done it up in a hurry, little tufts stuck out from under her hat, which kept its place badly, and her voluptuous grey eyes shone with a strange fire of lubricity, like two shining stars. She wore the look of a woman who had first enjoyed the caresses of a lover, and who may have made some show of resistance only to give herself away with a greater amount of abandonment. She had undoubtedly taken a late supper in some private room, and enjoyed the sweetmeats and the pastry on the sofa.

Already they had many stormy scenes on account of these late and frequent absences. He had even on several occasions gone the length of beating her in a most unmerciful manner, without producing any change in her conduct.

And yet this man loved his wife with all his heart. He had talked to her and treated her like a child, but the proud and magnificent Maud had treated him with scorn.

Once, however, as they were on the point of starting, — he was already in his dress clothes, and she, dressed all in pink silk, was standing before the cheval-glass occupied in hooking the clasp of a necklace of imitation pearls, it so happened that Brandon was abandoning himself to doleful thoughts and, thinking out loud. He said that no doubt she was pretty. Oh! of that he was sure! in this dress in which she looked like a lily in a rose. But it comes expensive, the silk and the making, and he was not rich, having barely £200 a year! And it would be necessary to diminish expenses, and not go so often to balls, if they wished to avoid falling soon into difficulties.

She turned round towards him, her cheeks flushing, a spark of anger in her eyes, and then in a sharp shrill voice that he had never yet heard from her, with her lip raised showing her little teeth, she began to speak very fast, after stamping her foot.

"Now you just listen. I intend to amuse myself. I did not get married to stick at home in a hole. If it does not please you, it's all the same to me. Let the ugly women hide themselves, that's quite right: I mean to show myself. After this ball, other balls; after this dress, other dresses. You may as well make up your mind to it. If it was a housekeeper you wanted, you should have hired one at so much a year. I am worth more than that. I have never told you so before; I tell it you now once for all! If you have not enough money, try to make some. I must have money, and more than I have ever yet had. I tell you beforehand; I don't deceive you. Borrow, get into debt, do what you like. Honest business if you can, or dishonest business. But understand this well, find money! If you cannot, all the worse for you, my boy! It is I who will find cash. Is that plain enough, eh? It's ten o'clock, come along."

She was already descending the stairs; he followed, amazed, stupefied. It was Maud who had spoken in these terms. He staggered from step to step, hurt and bruised as if he had received blows from a stick, or as if he had tumbled out of window.

✵✶

The ball took place at the house of the Count of Sainte-Galette, a wealthy man, a man who had long remained still young, who had filled a rather high situation in the French Ministry of Foreign affairs; and who, although a widower, gave evening parties where vaguely unclassed mundane ladies might be found, and where also were to be met with wives of government employés, anxious to procure the promotion of their husbands.

Brandon was stupefied, without a thought in his brain, and had not opened his mouth in the carriage, and when he entered the drawing-room full of noise and light, staggered like a drunken man. He wished almost to escape, to return home, but Maud was already whirling along the rosy train of her ball-dress in the mazes of the waltz with noisy rustle, and the poor man leaned against the wall, unperceived by the laughing and dancing crowd. He somehow found his way to another room, went still farther on, seeking instinctively for solitude, silence, and darkness; at last he pushed open another door, and fell down into an arm-chair.

He was alone, and in a rather small room, dimly lighted from above, and in which was a bed.

He could not help thinking of Maud. She was so gentle, so good, and yet so wicked, so atrociously wicked. He could well understand that his happiness was now wrecked, that he could no longer know the tenderness of tranquil love, the smiling little familiarities of home.

To this then had Maud descended. She so gentle, and now so cruel! So good, and so wicked! She would be sulky to him, would deceive him, would even quit him, as he had no more money to give her, and since she wanted money. Oh! money! There were others who worked less than he did, and who earned hundreds and thousands. On the Stock Exchange or in trade, or even by failing in business. He on the other hand, worked for eight hours a day in his studio, for £18 or £20 a month. How can one, with that, purchase dresses at twenty pounds a piece? And there must be no mistake; if he did not enrich himself, if he could not give to Maud all the luxury she wished for, he would lose her. Sometimes, seized with rage, he wanted to go back into the ball, to take hold of his wife's arm, to take her back to the house, to tear her fine toilette to pieces, to beat her, to say to her: "Now no more silk, that is all over.

"You must take to plain cotton, without trimming, and we shall dismiss the servant, and to-morrow morning you must do the household work, you shall mend my socks while I'm in my studio." For, after all, to mend socks, do household work, wear cotton dresses, that is the life that the honest wife of a poor man ought to lead. But he remembered that Maud had said to him: "If you cannot manage to find money, I will find it." And she would find it. She would therefore take a lover, — a rich lover! Ah! that was horrible and appalling. He knew her now. She would do as she had threatened to do, the wicked woman, he knew her now. She would do just as she had said. Therefore he must also earn big sums. Yes, he must. But how? By what means? He was only worth a place of sub-manager. He understood nothing at all of commercial business; he just knew enough to be sub-manager in a public office. Banknotes are not found wandering in the streets, and if you stroll along before Rothschild's bank you are not likely to have a chance of picking them up on the pavement! His elbows on his knees, he drove his fists into his temples, and at last, his mind on fire, his heart tortured, he began to sob despairingly, and — poor feeble man — began to stammer, "Money! Money! Money! for Maud!"

On raising his eyes, he saw before him a little writing-bureau, made of wood inlaid with mother-of-pearl. But why did he contemplate that piece of furniture? Without any object, without any reason, mechanically; the same as he looked at the lamp suspended from the ceiling, or the Chinese ornaments or the chimney.

He was still gazing at it, but more fixedly, and he noticed that the key, an extremely small key, was in the lock. That caused him at once pain and pleasure. The key was there. But in reality, he scarcely knew what he expected nor what he dreaded.

Something strange now occurred.

One of the folding doors of the escritoire, badly closed by a negligent hand, opened out slowly and widely, as if moved from within by an invisible power. The husband of Maud started up, gazing with eager eyes towards the opened piece of furniture.

On one of the shelves there was a pocket-book full of paper.

Brandon rushed to the writing-bureau, and opened the pocket-book with feverish hands.

It contained a mass of bank-notes: thirteen hundred or fourteen hundred pounds perhaps; enough money to buy Maud all the dresses she could wish for, enough money to ensure that she should never be false to him, that she should never abandon him! He trembled, a prey to the agonies of temptation. It came to his mind that he was alone, that nobody had seen him enter that room, that no one would see him leave it, that the robbery would not be discovered before three or four hours at least, that he would then be at home, that besides there were many people at this ball, that among so many persons it would be difficult to fix any suspicion. He thought that no one would ever suspect him, whose probity was known, and besides, it was not his fault after all. He had never thought of stealing anybody's money. It was the chiffonier, which opening, had suggested the idea to him. Why had this piece of furniture opened itself? Why was it opened, and who had pushed it open?

What unknown force offered suddenly to him, a poor man, riches? The real culprit would be chance. No doubt, he still resisted, because he was honest. He could not, he would not steal! Leaning forward, he was about to put back into the pocketbook the bundle of banknotes which he was rumpling in his hands. But the music of a waltz, which he heard through the half-opened doors, made him lose his presence of mind. His wife was dancing. With whom? With somebody, of whom she thought perhaps of becoming the mistress. He shoved all the banknotes into his pocket and turned towards the door.

All at once he stopped, he had heard the sound of steps on the carpet; some one approaching. He would be detected! He cast his eyes around; there was no other issue than the door through which the approaching persons would enter. Having lost his wits, he rushed into the nearest window recess, and concealed himself behind the curtains, risking a look between the fringes.

Those who now entered were Maud and the Count of Sainte-Galette, and hardly were they in the room when she cast her arms about his neck, laughing close to his lips. He was reading one of his latest amorous compositions:

> Maid of dark eyes that glow with shy sweet fire,
> Song lingers on thy beauty till it dies
> in awe and longing on the smitten lyre:
>   Maid of dark eyes.
>
> Grant me thy love, earth's last surpassing prize,
> Me, cast upon the faggots of love's pyre
> For love of the white bosom that underlies
>
> The subtle passion of thy snowy attire,
> The shadowy secret of thine amorous thighs,
> The inmost shrine of my supreme desire,
>   Maid of dark eyes!

⁕⁕

Oh! to rush on them, throw them down, strangle them, bite them! He was about to burst out, the curtains rustled. But then he began to tremble from head to foot, ready to faint.

He had the theft in his pocket! The banknotes swelled out his coat. No doubt, he could throw them away, hide them behind the hangings. But the chiffonier wide open, and the pocket-book open also and empty, that would be noticed, the Count would say: "I had money there. Where is it? Who has taken it? It is you." And all the guests would hurry up. He would be arrested. And for every one he would be a thief, a thief.

Maud, clinging to the neck of Count Sainte-Galette, was saying to him tender words; those words which intoxicate and bring smiles to the lips. It was indeed charming to be there, both together, so near to all the world, and yet so for; to be in the midst of a ball and yet to be alone; how she loved him, loved him entirely, as she had never loved before and would never love again. And the Count kissed her hair as she spoke, laughing and lovely.

All that, Brandon could hear and could see.

"It is much nicer here than in the hot ball-room," said Maud as she threw herself in an arm-chair.

"If I only had a glass of Champagne, I could be comfortable. But what would the waiter think if he found me here alone with you?"

"We can manage without his intervention," said the Count as he opened a cupboard and took out a bottle of champagne, two glasses, and a champagne knife. "A more important question is, what will your husband think if he should miss you?"

"Oh, he is never likely to miss me, and if he did he would not think of looking for me here. But you might as well shut that door."

"What a thoughtful little woman you are," said the Count. He put down the bottle of Champagne, walked across the room, and locked the door. Then he returned, picked up the bottle again, and began to take off the wire.

"I see you understand opening champagne," said Maud.

"Oh, that's not the only sort of thing I open in this room," replied the Count, smiling at her lasciviously, and then glancing at the bed.

Maud stretched out her dainty foot and gave him a little kick. "I expect you find it easier, to open the champagne than the — other thing," she said.

The cork flew out with a loud pop, and the Count deftly poured the foaming amber liquid into two large goblets, one of which he handed her with a bow, and then came and sat down on the chair beside her. "You have seen how well I open champagne," he said, "would you like to see how well I can open —"

"A girl's legs?" she replied quickly. "Well, I suppose I must let you. For I see you want a bit," and she rose and began to take off her dress. In a few moments she stood before him in only her chemise and drawers. "I was not going to have my dress spoiled," she added, "and at any rate you will have to give me another. Beside, I know you like me better without my clothes."

"Of course I do, darling," replied the Count. "You shall have all the dresses you want, as long as you take them off when you come to me."

"Very well," said Maud, "don't let us waste any time. How are you going to have me? Lying on the bed, or astride on your knees, or from behind?"

Before the Count could answer, Brandon who could contain himself no longer, had thrown aside the curtain and bounded into the room. He seized his wife by the arm and threw her from him violently.

"You miserable whore," he cried, "I do not know what prevents me from killing you and your vile paramour together. Put on your clothes at once, and come along home with me. To-morrow I will consider what I shall do to you. As for you," he added, turning to the Count, "you may thank your stars that you are in your own house. As it is, two of my friends shall wait on you in the morning. Dueling is forbidden in England, but there are plenty of places outside Calais or Boulogne where I suppose you could have no objection to meet me, and, since I am debarred from the pleasure of knocking you down, let me at least have the satisfaction of putting a bullet into you."

The Count who was a man of the world, rose to his feet and bowed stiffly.

"It shall be as you wish, sir," he said quietly; "your friends will find me here, and if you consider I owe you any reparation, I shall be happy to give it." Suddenly he started, and then added, "In the meantime, sir, I should be glad to know how it is that my purse is in your hand."

Brandon looked at him blankly, and then he remembered, and he tossed the purse from him as though it had been a poisonous snake. He tottered to a chair, fell into it, and strong man though he was, he sobbed aloud.

The Count looked at him pityingly for a few moments, then he walked up to Brandon, and laid his hand on the painter's shoulder.

"I can see how it is, my poor fellow," he said kindly. "You love that woman," and he glanced at Maud who was lying in a swoon on the sofa.

"You love her so much that for her sake, and that you may supply her with everything that her extravagant nature demands, you have not hesitated to take money that did not belong to you."

"Yes," replied Brandon; "I loved her so much that I would have sacrificed anything — even my own honour — for her sake, but my love for her has gone, for I see now that she no longer cares for me, and that you have her affection."

"My dear fellow," said the Count, "she cares absolutely nothing for me, except for the one reason that I can give her money to satisfy her extravagant wants." He stooped down, and whispered in Brandon's ear, "Have you a riding-whip at home?"

Brandon did not understand the question, but he nodded affirmatively.

"Well, then, take her home," whispered the Count; "tie her up to the bed-post, and with a whip, or cane, or, better still, a birch rod, give her a sound flogging — make her smart well, but don't be too cruel, and I think you will find that will not only cure her of gadding about after other men, but will restore to both of you the love and affection you both had when you first married. Try it, and I think you will be glad you followed my advice."

Brandon nodded, but could not reply, and at that moment Maud opened her eyes, and looked wildly round. When she saw her husband sitting at the other side of the room, with his face buried in his hands, she began to sob again, but she rose from the couch and mechanically began to put on her petticoats and dress.

The Count did not say a word, but as soon as he saw she was dressed, he left the room, and returned in a minute or two with her cloak, which he helped her to put on. Her husband took her arm, and after bowing to the Count, led her out of the room and downstairs. The Count had sent one of the footmen for a cab, which was now at the door. Maud looking half dazed, entered the cab, and Brandon having told the driver the address, entered the vehicle, which started off at that jog trot peculiar to the London growler.

Neither Maud nor Brandon spoke for some time. At last she asked, "Are you going to fight the Count?"

"Perhaps," replied Brandon. "Would it grieve you very much if I killed him?"

"No," she retorted angrily, "I wish you would both kill each other. I hate both of you. He gives me money, but he can only paw me about, and you who can satisfy me, have no money."

At this moment the cab drew up at the door of their little house in Chelsea. Brandon dismissed the cab, and opened the door with his latch-key. Maud entered the house, and her husband having locked the door, lighted a candle and motioned to his wife to ascend the stairs. The servant had gone to bed, knowing that her master could let himself in.

HOW A WIFE WAS THRASHED

MAN demands unconditional fidelity from his wife, but does not concede to her the right to demand the same from him. When she forgets herself, she has committed a deadly sin, whose lightest penalty is public contempt; when he does the same, he has only been guilty of a charming little lapse from duty for which the law has no penalty, at which society smiles discreetly and good-naturedly, and which the wife pardons with tears and caresses if she took it seriously in the first place. And the unfairness of this dual standard is increased by the circumstance that in reality it is not the same whether the husband or the wife is guilty of infidelity: for if the wife sins, she is passive in the matter led astray by a man, that is, a power independent of her will; she succumbs to a force which is stronger than her powers of resistance; but when the husband sins he is not passive; he sins because he wishes to sin; there are very few Josephs outside of the Bible, and the wife of Potiphar is a rarity; the man takes the initiative in sin, he goes in quest of it, and commits it with concentrated purpose and premeditation, with energy and in spite of the resistance offered to him.

The excitement and revulsion of feeling had been so great, that Brandon felt so hot and stifled that he could scarcely breathe. The first thing he did on entering the bedroom was to lock the door, and then he hastily threw off his dress-suit and boots.

Maud stood in the middle of the room, and gazed at

him with a half-terrified expression. "You are not going to kill me?" she asked in frightened tones.

"No, I am not," he replied, "though you richly deserve it." He stopped in front of her and looked at her dress. "I suppose your lover paid for that," he said; "take it off at once."

She did not obey at once, and he roughly stripped off her dress and all other garments except her stockings and shoes. He then went into his dressing room and returned with a long piece of rope, which he securely fastened round one of her wrists. Then he made her put one arm on each side of the bed-post and fastened both wrists together. She looked at him appealingly, but did not venture to resist. He fetched a handkerchief, and tied it securely over her mouth to prevent her screams being heard. Finally he opened a cupboard, and hesitated for some time whether he should select a riding whip, a Malacca cane, or a leather strap, for it need not be said that having never anticipated that he would need a birch rod, he had never supplied himself with that valuable adjunct to the happiness of married life. He at last decided upon the leather strap; and having picked it up, he returned to Maud, who was sobbing as loudly as her gagged condition would permit.

"Now, Maud, I am going to flog some of the lust out of you," said Brandon.

He passed his hand over her smooth, white, firm, well-rounded buttocks. Like most English husbands he had never seen his wife naked, but he had seen many naked models in his studio, and they had never caused any lascivious thoughts in his mind, nor did Maud's charms now, though they would have tempted a saint to break his vow of chastity.

Brandon had nothing on but his shirt and drawers. He rolled his shirt sleeves up to the elbow, and then raising his arm, he brought the strap down smartly on the left cheek of Maud's splendid bottom. It instantly flushed a rosy red, and Maud writhed her beautiful body in pain, and tried to scream, but she was so effectually gagged that only a hoarse groan escaped her. Again the strap rose and fell, and Maud's right buttock blushed as rosily as its sister.

Brandon continued to deal his strokes methodically, and at each blow a broad white band appeared on the pink surface, and then disappeared, and Maud twisted and wriggled her bottom about, and sometimes she would open her legs and show the "spot" for a moment, and then her quivering thighs would close again and shut out the charming spectacle, and her feet would jump off the floor with pain.

Maud's struggles at last caused the handkerchief that gagged her to fall to the ground, and she screamed out, "For mercy's sake undo me. Enough! I'll do nothing bad again." Her pleadings only made him more determined, and with a swish in the air he again brought the strap down, making her twist about with fear and shame. "You hussy," said her husband, "I'll make you drag my name through the mud and get me laughed at. Take that and that," and then, seizing the whip, in his anger he struck her several smart blows where the strap had already fallen leaving large weals to mark its fierce passage.

Maud was a grandly made woman, and the contortions of her body as she skipped from side to side to avoid the fast-descending blows would have made an anchorite rage with lust. No man can witness the finely modelled arse of a lovely woman plunging about before his eyes without undergoing certain physiological changes, even though that woman brought him serious wrong. We are after all only flesh and blood, as the omniscient Gladstone once said under vastly different circumstances, in the English House of Commons. This scene of domestic correction was once more to prove the truth of that very trite adage.

Brandon became aware that a curious psychological change was being effected in him, and that his feelings towards his erring wife had radically changed. He had resolved that he would never touch her again after she had so cruelly deceived him. He would sue for a divorce, and until that was procured he would never occupy the same bed with her, but before the strap had fallen for the sixth time he began to think how beautiful she was, and to remember how often he had pressed her fair body in those love battles in which each had been the conqueror, and each delighted to be the vanquished. He determined not to give way to these tender thoughts, and only remember her heartlessness and deceit, and four times more did the strap descend upon her bottom, but though it quivered and trembled at each blow, Maud no longer wriggled as she had done, and did not attempt to scream.

He was afraid that she had fainted, and throwing down the strap, he looked anxiously at her face. She had not fainted, in fact her face was suffused with a beautiful blush, and her eyes which glittered strangely, were fixed on some object. He followed their direction, and saw that his tool had come through the opening of his drawers and was standing in all the magnificence of a full erection.

"Poor little woman," he thought to himself, "how she would like to have that in her belly, and how much I should like to put it there, but I cannot honourably do so now. At all events, I won't beat her any more."

He removed the handkerchief which gagged her, and expected that the first use she made of her tongue would be to overwhelm him with abuse and recriminations, but to his surprise, as soon as the gag was removed she said:

"Make haste and undo me, darling."

He quickly unfastened the cord, and she stood upright and faced him. He thought he had never seen her look so lovely. Her body quivered with excitement and her eyes gleamed with lust. Her magnificent breasts rose and fell beneath her panting breath.

"Oh, Robert, how I love you!" she cried.

She sprang towards him and threw her right arm round his neck. She pressed her warm sensuous lips to his, and darted her tongue into his mouth. At the same instant she gripped his tool with her left hand, and threw herself back on the bed. The movement was so sudden and unexpected that he lost his footing and fell with her, and before he had time to think of what she was doing, she had pressed the head of his prick between the gaping lips of her coynte, and thrown her legs round his thighs.

> O large lips opening outward like a flower
> To breathe upon my face that clings to thee!
> O wanton breasts that heave deliciously
> And tempt my eager teeth! O cruel power
> Of wide deep thighs that make me furious
> As they enclasp me and swing to and fro
> With passion that grows pale and drive the flow
> Of the fast fragrant blood of both of us
> Into the awful link that knits us close
> With chain electric! O have mercy yet
> In drawing out my life in this desire
> To consummate this moment all the gross
> Lusts of to-night, and pay the sudden debt
> That with strong water shall put out our fire!

Brandon had determined never to forgive her, but when a man's breast is being pressed by a pair of the largest and softest bubbies in the world, when a pretty woman's tongue is in his mouth, and a charming coynte is eagerly sucking in his hot and burning tool, resolves of that sort do not count for much. Brandon did what any vigorous young man would have done under similar circumstances and putting his arms round her waist, with one powerful lunge, he buried his resentment and the whole of his tool in Maud's heaving belly.

Maud, as we have already said, was a magnificent creature, and though Brandon was furnished with an instrument which would have terrified many a woman, she met every one of his strong lunges with an upheaval of her buttocks which were still burning with the lust created by the beneficent strap, and not until she felt his purse against the lips of her coynte did she cease to press forward. They lay motionless, and as in a swoon, until the warm life-giving fluid bathed their whole being in a flood of ecstatic delight. Then her limbs relaxed, and Brandon withdrew his now limp tool, and rolled off her.

He dreamily watched Maud get out of bed, and go and wash herself, and take off her shoes and stockings which she had still worn when he flogged her.

When she had finished, she came and stood by the side of the bed, and looked down at him roguishly.

"Bob, dear," she said, "do you forgive me?"

"I suppose I must," he replied. "I didn't intend to, but you have such taking ways."

She laughed. "You see I can take all you have to give me, and as often as you like. In fact I should like a bit more now if you are ready to give it me, but I suppose you will want tickling up a little before you are ready."

She put her hand inside the opening of his drawers and laid hold of his tool.

"Oh, this will never do," she said laughingly. "Why it is all limp like a big worm. Get out of bed at once, sir, and let me put you into the proper condition to present yourself before a lady."

He obeyed her and jumped off the bed.

"First let us have this nasty shirt off," she said, and her nimble fingers began to undo his collar. "You finish that," she continued, "whilst I go to the bathroom to fetch some warm water, and remember that when I come back I shall expect to find you stripped, *quite* stripped. Do you hear, Bob?"

She slipped on a black silk dressing-gown, and taking the candle, left the room.

Poor Brandon felt in a rather difficult position. Not an hour ago he had determined to cast off his wife and never see her again, and yet almost as soon as he had made that resolution, he had rogered her, and he was bound to confess that he had never enjoyed a futter so much in his life.

Indeed, though she had only gone out of the room for a minute, he longed for her to return and conduct him once more to pleasures such as he had never believed mortals could enjoy.

He heard her footsteps returning. "She mustn't find me like this," he said to himself, and he quickly threw off his shirt and drawers and stood quite naked. "It's all your fault," he added looking down at the limp tool dangling between his legs; "you can't let a slit come near you but what you must plunge into it headlong, and a nice fool you've made your master look in consequence. I don't know that I can blame you for it though, for you gave me a great deal of pleasure, and, in fact, if you like to begin again I don't think I should scold you. But you don't look fit at present."

"I haven't been long, have I?" said Maud as she entered the room, "but I was obliged to get some warm water, for with cold I should never have got my dear little friend to put his head up. Ah, I see you have done as I told you. That's right! Now come here and let me see to you," and she poured some warm water into a basin, and kneeling on the carpet in front of her husband, she washed his tool and dried it with a soft towel.

"Oh, Maud," cried Brandon, "I don't like to see you doing this."

"Why not?" she replied. "It worked so well for me just now that I'm sure it deserves a little attention. Look! it's half stiff already. What a nice, tight purse you have, Bob. You know the story of the blind girl who asked if that didn't go in too? Well! I really believed just now that yours was going in. I know I tried my best to get it in."

"I know you did, darling, and so did I," replied Brandon. "But I wish for your sake that it was a purse of money."

"It is better than money, Bob," said Maud. "I am not going to be extravagant any more except in one respect."

"And what is that?" he asked.

"Why I am going to make you spend — that is the proper word too — all that you have in this purse," — and she weighed it in her hand — "on me — literally *on* me."

"Oh, Maud, you are a duck," cried Brandon. "I am so sorry I beat you just now."

"On the contrary I am very glad," said Maud. "You did not hurt me much, and it is nearly well now. Look," and she threw off her dressing gown, and stooping down showed her bottom, from which the marks had disappeared, but which was still of a bright pink colour which afforded a pretty contrast to the dazzling white of her back and thighs. "No, I didn't ask you to touch it, sir, and least of all to put your hand between my legs. Besides, you silly boy, didn't you know that there is nothing makes a woman so randy as a good flogging, and nothing so much excites a man as flogging a woman or seeing her flogged? If it had not been for that beating I should never have had the best rogering you have ever given me, and which I think, sir," she continued mischievously, "you enjoyed quite as much as I did."

"I have heard about it before," said Brandon, "but I must say I never believed in it. Besides, a man would be a brute who would flog a woman every time he wanted to get into her, and let her have all the pain whilst he had all the pleasure."

"Oh, but there's a better way," said Maud, "by which a man and a girl can halve the pain and double the pleasure."

"And what is that?" he asked.

"Why, though it makes a man stand to see a woman receive a flogging, it gives him a still stronger erection when he gets a few cuts on his own bottom."

"Well," said Brandon with a laugh, "I don't think I've had my bottom flogged since I was a schoolboy, but it is but fair that I should be served with the same sauce as I served you, so if you'd like to try the effect of a few cuts on my backside, blaze away little woman, but I warn you that I don't believe in your method."

Maud smiled. "At any rate I shall take precautions," and she placed two pillows, one on the top of the other in the centre of the bed. "At any rate too you must acknowledge that your present condition is not satisfactory," and she pointed to his tool which was quite limp. "Now then, Bob dear, put your head against the side of the bed."

Brandon obeyed, and Maud picked up the strap and brought it down smartly across his buttocks.

"Oh, I say," ejaculated her husband, "that stings more than I thought it would. I don't like it."

"Screw your courage up, and don't be afraid. I won't hurt you more than I can help, and won't give you a cut more than is necessary."

A second time the strap descended, and wielded as it was by Maud's vigorous arm, it made Brandon jump about, and at a third he could not suppress an oath. Maud put her arm round under his belly and felt his tool.

"It doesn't seem to have had any effect as yet," she said. "Of course not," replied her husband testily; "what is the use of hurting me for nothing?"

Maud made no reply but brought the strap down three times more, and again slipped her hand under his belly.

"It is nearly stiff now," she cried, "a couple more will do it."

Twice more she brought down the strap, and then quickly skipped out of his way, as Brandon stood upright, faced round with his magnificent engine boldly rearing its huge red head, and tried to grasp her. With a merry laugh she ran quickly round the bed, and with one bound she was lying on it. She had barely time to place her bottom on the pillows, and stretch open her arms and legs before Brandon had thrown himself on the top of her, and had levelled his dart at her love-nest. The mark was easy enough to hit, and in another moment her arms and legs were clasped round him and he was driving into her with long strokes, each of which caused her to give a grunt of pleasure.

The strokes grew shorter but Maud met every heave of his powerful loins unflinchingly, and with her hands grasping the cheeks of his still smarting bottom and her firm white muscular legs crossed over the back of his thighs, she pressed him so tightly that the whole of his enormous engine was buried up to the roots, and still her insatiable coynte was unsatisfied.

"Tell me when you're coming, darling," she whispered, "and we'll both go off together."

"Now! Now!" he cried half a minute later, and Maud, letting go his bottom, clasped her long white arms round his back, and met every one of his short sharps digs with a furious wriggle of her bottom.

The two splendid bodies seemed melted into one, so closely were they united. Then a long shivering spasm passed through them, and Brandon rolled off breathless and exhausted, his neck bleeding from a bite which Maud's sharp little teeth had inflicted in the supreme moment.

After resting for a minute or two, he got out of bed and washed himself, and then picking up the candle which had been left burning, he came to the bed and gazed down at Maud. She had not moved since he got off her, and was lying, with her eyes closed in a half swoon of ecstatic pleasure. The two pillows which she had thoughtfully placed to raise her buttocks, gave a graceful curve to her lithe while body. Her arms were thrown above her head, and her thighs were still wide apart. The light of the candle fell on the golden hair under her armpits, on the red nipples, which surmounted her two big, soft breasts, and on the forest which covered her well-developed mount of Venus, beneath which could be seen the half open pink "big lips" of her vulva, still moist with the love stream which Brandon had shot into her.

"If I could only paint her like that, what a splendid picture it would be!" he said to himself. He put his head between her thighs, and gently kissed the place which had given him so much pleasure. She opened her eyes and smiled at him sweetly. "What! not satisfied yet, you bad boy?" she said. "And kissing my poor little quim in that hypocritical manner after knocking her about and then flooding her. But she is a good fighter, and you will find her ready to meet your champion as often as he can get ready for the battle."

She got off the bed and limped to the wash-stand, "You have stretched me so much with that big machine of yours that you have made me quite lame," she said.

"Yes, I was afraid it would hurt you!" said Brandon, "I have never poked you like that since we were married."

"Well, that wasn't my fault," she replied laughingly. "It was always there ready for you. But you are like all the men. They think that if they give their wives dresses and jewellery that is all we want, and if once a week they give us a hurried grind we ought to be satisfied, and if a man does know how to poke a woman properly — which very few do — he reserves all his talents for his mistress, because he thinks she knows how to do it better."

"To be sure," she added, "many wives are also to blame. All they think of is their husband's dinner, whereas if they thought less of his belly and more of what was below it, there would be more happy couples."

There is no need to describe in detail the rest of this eventful night, suffice it to say that, thanks to the flagellation, and a little skilful aid from Maud's hand and tongue, Brandon was enabled to get off a couple more turns before he fell asleep by his wife's side.

Even this did not complete his performance, for when he woke in the morning his tool was stiff, as is usually the case with a man in good health. Maud was lying on her back fast asleep, and quite naked, and looked so lovely and tempting in the morning light that he would have been unworthy of the name of man if he had not taken advantage of the chance.

He gently pulled apart her big, firm, well-rounded thighs, and then kneeling between them, opened the soft pink lips of her rosy love-cleft with his fingers and inserted the head of his huge tool. Maud was probably awake all the time, but she took care not to open her eyes till he had quietly pushed more than half the big red column into the soft, warm, wet receptacle. Then she pretended to wake with a start. "What, again!" she cried with well feigned surprise. "Well, it's lucky I am a good strong girl, and can take a good deal of grinding, for I do not think there are many women who could stand five assaults in one night from such a huge machine as you have. But if you will take it out, Bob, I will show you a new way which I think will please you, and which not many women, even professionals, can do."

"You won't trick me if I take it out?" said her husband.

"Of course not, you silly boy! I like it just as much as you do, or perhaps more, but you are very heavy, and your long strokes drive all the breath out of me."

"All right, little woman, I don't want to hurt you, so what do you want me to do?"

"Why, get off — that's it — and now lie flat on your back in the middle of the bed."

Brandon did as he was told, and lay down as directed, his grand tool — superbly stiff from being interrupted when it was half way to its goal, lying straight against his belly.

Maud's eyes glistened with pleasure as she looked at it. "You are a beauty, my dear," she said, as she caressed it with her hand, and bent down her pretty face and gave it a little kiss on its big, red, proudly swelling head. "It seems quite a pity to spoil you and make you all limp, but I don't think you much mind that."

"You'll take all the stiffness out of it quicker than you intended, Maud, if you keep on handling it. Make haste and slip it in, darling, or I shall think you are afraid of it."

"I'll soon show you whether I am afraid of it, sir," replied Maud, and she threw one leg over his body and knelt on the bed with one leg each side of him. Then, putting her left hand round behind her thigh, she caught hold of his tool and pulled it up straight. Next, with her right hand she held apart the lips of her sweet rosy cleft, and gently lowered her body till the big head of the great column had disappeared.

"Now remember, Bob," she said with mock gravity, and holding up her finger, "you are not to move. I daresay you will want to shove it in further, but you must conquer the inclination or you will spoil the game."

"All right," he replied. "I will do whatever you want — if I can."

Maud continued to lower her body until about two thirds of his prickle had entered her.

"That will do," she cried. "If your old pet were not so

long I could let it all in, but now it is just right. Do you feel anything darling?"

"Yes," he replied, "I can feel something tickling the tip of my tool most deliciously."

"That is my clitty playing round it. Now do you feel anything?"

"Yes; my old man is being squeezed and pressed and sucked as though it were in your mouth. What have you got inside there, Maud?"

A lady who had travelled in Turkey told me that some of the Turks have in their harems women who are called nutcrackers, who can make a man spend by working the muscles of their vulva. She taught me how to do it and I used to practise — only with a candle, of course — but I wasn't sure I could do it, but I never told you anything about it because — I was — afraid — you wouldn't respect me."

"Respect you, darling!" he replied. "When I think that I have been night after night lying close to the cleverest little coynte in all England and never found out its beauties, I could kick myself. This is heavenly."

He closed his eyes and seemed lost in ecstasy, whilst Maud knelt astride him apparently motionless, though all the muscles of her vulva were at work squeezing, gripping, sucking, and exciting the pleasant intruder who had ventured into that nest of delight. "Maud! I'm co — co — coming," he murmured at last.

She, her eyes gleaming with lust, opened her legs, and gave a downward thrust which made all the rest of the great column disappear into her widely gaping, insatiable coynte, and throwing her body upon his, lay motionless with her warm mouth to his, her very being melted in the warm flood of love which was being spurted into her womb.

They lay thus for some minutes, and then his now limp tool slipped out of her cleft, and Maud, with a merry laugh, got off him, though he tried to retain her.

"No, no," she said, "that is quite enough for the

present. I shall have you knocking yourself up, and unable to do anything for a month, and now you have begun so well I hope you will continue."

"You shall see," he cried. "Oh, Maud darling, I love you better than ever, and yet last night I felt as though I could have killed you."

"Well, sir," she replied with a laugh, "I think you did your best. Five times! And your great thing is fully nine inches long! That makes nearly four feet of tool that you drove with all your might into my poor little belly. You have stretched me so that I shall be hardly able to walk for a day or two. But at any rate I have convinced you of the merits of flagellation."

"Oh, yes, I acknowledge that," he said. "It is very efficacious — but I think I like the nut-cracking best. Maud dear," he whispered confidentially, "you're not too modest, are you dear, to let me *see* what you did that with?"

Maud blushed.

"It's not much good either of us pretending to be modest," she replied, "when we're both of us stark naked, and making no attempt to hide what we've each got, but I don't intend to let you peep inside my slit all the same."

"Why not?" he asked.

"Because you would be obliged to touch it to look inside, and then you would want to put something else besides your finger in."

"Oh, no, I promise I wouldn't. Besides," he added dolefully, "you have taken it down so effectually, that I *couldn't* if I wanted to."

"Well, I suppose I must, if you insist," said Maud, and sitting on the edge of the bed, he threw her body back, and opened her thighs as wide as ever they would go.

Brandon came and knelt between her legs, and admired the rich forest of curly golden hair. Then with his fingers he gently opened the big lips, and made a long and careful inspection of the interior. When he had finished, he bestowed a long loving kiss on "the mouth with no teeth," and rose to his feet.

"You're a sweetly pretty girl, Maud," he said, "and that isn't the least pretty part about you. But I am as wise as I was before!"

Well, if you've quite done rummaging my secret charms," said Maud, "we'll have breakfast."

Thanks to Maud's receptive and nut-cracking capabilities, and Brandon's fine proportioned "lady-killer," the reconciliation which was the outcome of this night of delirious lust was complete and lasting, but Brandon was absurdly jealous, and always imagined that his wife would some day cease to be satisfied with the amount of rogering he was able to give her, and would seek in the arms of other men to assuage her passions.

In this he wronged her, for though Maud was of a warm, amorous full-blooded nature, and could easily have taken more than her husband gave her; though he thoroughly appreciated her charms and was more liberal of his embraces than ever — she was not lascivious, nor likely to deceive a husband whom she knew did the best he could, merely to gratify sensual passions.

Brandon, however, could not realise this, and partly that he might be always with her and undisturbed by society, he took a house in a small village in Scotland.

There they lived happily some months; indeed Brandon would have been hard to please if he had not been satisfied with the skilful love-making of Maud, who was always ready for his assaults, and was continually devising fresh methods, each of which seemed better than the last to entranced Brandon.

He made sketches in the neighbourhood, and some

of these sketches attracted the attention of a riche amateur, who gave him a commission to execute a series of views of Swiss scenery. Brandon was very far from being a rich man, and he found that it would be impossible for him to take Maud with him.

"It will be awfully lonely for me," said Maud, "and when I think that I shall not feel your big baton between my legs for three or four months, I could cry. But there is no help for it, and I promise you on my word of honour that I will wait for your return and live quite chastely all the time. I will not ask the same of you, for I know what men are, and they have laid down the comfortable theory that a married man may go with as many women as he likes, but a married woman must have no one but her husband. So I expect you will put your big machine into a good many pretty Swiss girls before you come back."

"My dear Maud," said her husband, "that is a popular delusion about the Swiss girls, they are, as a rule, abominably ugly, but if they were not I should not touch them, for I could never hope to meet one as pretty as you, or as good a poke."

Whether Brandon kept his word is very doubtful, but he certainly never found any Swiss girl who was to be compared to Maud, and he was heartily glad when his last sketch was finished and he could return home, more especially as he had received a letter from Maud only a day or two before to say that she was very tired of sleeping alone, and that she had laid in a nice stock of birch rods.

Moreover she added that her crackers were in good working order, and able to crack his nut as often as he could put it there.

He was therefore looking forward to a pleasurable time, and had hurried home as fast as he could. But few of his friends even knew he was married, and he had pretended to his friend Lawrence that it was no petticoat business that had brought him to England

and was taking him to Scotland.

Therefore when he took his place in the train his mind was still running on Maud, and the woman sitting opposite to him still further excited his sexual passions. He had not had a woman for at least three weeks, but he had committed so many infidelities that one or two more or less did not affect his conscience.

We have already seen what occurred between them until the time the train drew up with a sharp jerk, and had thrown the lady into his arms, and we will now continue the history from the moment at which we left it.

BEAUTY AND THE BEAST

THE LADY FAINTS AWAY
ON HER BACK AND THAT WHICH
HAPPENED TO HER IN THAT VERY
NATURAL POSITION

EMILE Zola, that clever French novel-writer and scatophile, in a book which has become famous, *La Terre* (The Soil), draws a fine picture of a scene of rape with violence.

It was in the month of October on a mild, damp day. The actors in this little drama were peasants. The rape took place in a field. Buteau was the brother-in-law of the woman he raped. The latter lived in his house with him and her sister, and aided them both in their field, and other occupations. The violated girl had a lover named Jean, who was very fond of her, and who came furtively now and again to see her. They contemplated marriage. Owing to misunderstandings with regard to the division of the family patrimony, Françoise did not get on very well with her brother-in-law and sister. They made her life in their house a little hell, and although she did not much care for her sweetheart, Jean, she intended to marry him as soon as possible to escape their tyranny. Buteau hated Jean, because the latter had once thrashed him and broken his arm. Readers who desire further details concerning the actors of this wonderful romance should study the book for themselves. We have discovered that the English edition of "La Terre" does not give a full, verbatim account of the French original, but, on the contrary omits the smartest, and of course, most interesting parts, which we deeply deplore.

"What had put Buteau into such a savage temper was, that while bringing his harrow back, he had seen Jean and Françoise hurrying away behind a wall. The girl, who had gone out on the pretence of getting some grass for her cows, had not yet returned, for she knew what kind of reception awaited her. The night was already falling, and Buteau, in a furious rage, went out every minute into the yard, and even on to the road, to see if the hussy were coming back. He swore at the top of his voice, and poured out a torrent of filthy language, without observing old Fouan, who was sitting on the stone bench, calming himself after the row, and enjoying the warm softness of the air, which made that sunny October like a spring month.

"The sound of clogs was heard coming up the slope, and Françoise made her appearance, bending double, for her shoulders were laden with an enormous bundle of grass, which she had tied up in an old cloth. She was panting and perspiring, almost hidden beneath her burden.

"'Ah! you blasted street-runner!' cried Buteau, 'do you think to make game of me, getting yourself polished off for the last two hours by your Jock, when there's work to be done here!'

"And tumbling her over on to the bundle of grass which had fallen down, he threw himself upon her just as Lisa, in her turn, was leaving the house with the intention of blackguarding him furiously.

"'Eh! Mary shit-the-bed, come along here, that I may kick your arse!... You're not ashamed of yourself!' she cried.

"But Buteau had already seized hold of the girl under her petticoats, with both hands. His rage turned always to a sudden rush of lust. While he was trussing her up on the grass, he growled like a beast, half-choked, his face violet and blood-swollen.

"'You damned whore, it's got to be my turn, now... Though God's thunder burst, you'll have to go through it after t'other chap!'

"Then there was a furious struggle. Old Fouan could not see very well in the darkness. But he could still distinguish Lisa standing up, looking on, and letting matters go; while her man, wallowing, and thrust aside every second or two, was exhausting himself in vain, but still satisfying himself as well as he could, anyhow, no matter where.

"When it was done, Françoise managed with a last effort to get free, and then, choking and stuttering, she shouted:

"'You beast! you beast! you beast!... You couldn't do it, that doesn't count... I don't care a rap! but you shall never have me, never!'

"She had triumphed; she took a wisp of grass, and wiped her leg, her whole body trembling the while, as if she were rather satisfied than otherwise at the obstinacy of her refusal. With a gesture of bravado, she threw the wisp of grass at her sister's feet.

"'Here, this belongs to you; it's not your fault if I give it you back!'

"But Buteau had not yet given up the game.

"He called out to his wife:

"You blasted lazy bitch! What's the use of your idly looking on?.. Why can't you help; catch hold of her legs, if you want me to do the job.'"

"Lisa stood aloof, motionless, some ten yards away, casting her eyes far away, and then bringing them back upon the couple before her, without a muscle of her face betraying the least emotion.

"But now that she was called upon by her husband, she showed not a moment's hesitation, and stepping forward seized hold of her sister's left leg, stretched it apart and sat herself upon it as if she had a mind to crush it. Françoise, nailed to the ground, gave herself up, her nerves broken, and her eyelids closed. But she retained full consciousness, and when Buteau had indeed possessed her, she was herself in her turn carried away in such a sharp voluptuous spasm, that she passionately clasped both her arms round his neck fit to choke him, giving forth a long convulsive cry."

The history of rape is the history of humanity itself. Wherever man has found woman, he has sought by fair means or foul to throw her over on her back, and in nine cases out of ten woman has been content to rest there until the man has vigorously frictioned her. Between the white thighs of the woman is the most wonderful thing that has ever tempted man. To gain its favours he has run frightful risks and ventured his all; fortune, reputation and even his life. When, in the Twentieth Century, history comes to be written without fear, mystery or falsehood, the recital of the virgins violated, the matrons taken by force, and even of old women sacrificed to unbridled lust, will excite the pity and indignation of soberer mankind. The wonder of it all is that while women have always dreaded the penis-thrusts of the male, they have been unable in the majority of cases even when taken by force, to avoid sharing the fierce joy of the orgasm thereby produced. From the fresh-faced servant girl slung on her back in the kitchen, to the haughty-browed queen, futtered in the shadow of the throne, history teaches the one lesson of the persistent fascination and subserviency of the Coynte of woman to the imperious needs of man.

It is time now to return to the ardent painter and reluctant lady playing at hide and seek in the train.

When the train pulled up with such a sudden jerk, Brandon was at first inclined to suppose that an accident had taken place, and apparently the same thought had struck the lady, for the pistol dropped from her grasp, and she appeared to have swooned.

His first act was to lift her veil and look at her face, which he found to be even more beautiful than he had anticipated. Her beauty was of quite a different type to Maud, and he was well aware that even if he should bring the adventure to a favourable termination he was not likely to find his new acquaintance such an adept in the pleasing sports of love as his wife was, but at any rate she was certainly very pretty, and he judged from her conduct that she would be quite as willing to feel his standing tool lodged between her thighs as he was to put it there, for he believed that the revolver which had fallen from her grasp was only a trick to try him, and that if he had been really frightened by it she would probably have been more disappointed than he would.

He was still holding her in his arms, when a light flashed in his eyes. He looked down and saw that it proceeded from the lantern carried by the guard, who was walking up the line to the engine to find out what was the matter.

It flashed across Brandon's mind that he must look rather peculiar holding a woman in his arms, but it would have made matters worse if he had shouted out an explanation, which would have been overheard in the next carriage; besides it did not really matter, for the guard would not know that they were not a newly-married couple.

He, however, gently placed the lady on a seat, and when a couple of minutes later the guard came back again he asked what was the matter?

"It's all right, sir," replied the official. "A truck came detached from a goods train and got on the main line, but it was seen, and the signal set against us just in time, but we had to pull up pretty sharp. The line is being cleared and we shall go on again in a minute."

In fact at that moment a sharp whistle came from the engine, and the guard who appeared to be about to say something more, hurried back as fast as he could to his van.

Brandon turned once more to the lady, who still appeared to be in a swoon. He pressed his burning lips to hers, but she did not open her eyes. He began to be a little bit frightened, and thought the best thing to do would be to open her dress. He did so and disclosed a neck white as alabaster, and a bosom covered by a fine chemise trimmed with lace. He pulled this down as far as he could, and brought to view two small but beautifully round breasts, just showing their little pink nipples above the corset which confined them.

He would have been more than mortal if he could have refrained from kissing these soft white warm globes, the very touch of which sent an electric thrill all through him.

The lady sighed, but still her eyes did not open, and one of her feet dropped to the ground.

Brandon who was kneeling by her side, had not seen many women faint, but he thought that in the stillness of unconsciousness she looked even more beautiful than when her eyes were open.

Whilst he was still gazing at her, he was glad to hear the whistle of the engine, and feel the train once more move on. He had made up his mind to possess this woman, but he guessed that if she should come to and find herself being raped, she would struggle and scream. If the train were going at full speed her cries would not be heard amidst the loud rattle and din made by the express, but, of course, it would be madness to attempt to violate her whilst the train was standing still, as her cries would bring the guard and some of the passengers to her assistance, and not only would he be unable to effect his purpose, but he would certainly be arrested, and in all probability sentenced to a long term of imprisonment, rape being an offence which the judges regard as one of the most serious offences which a man can commit.

It was therefore a relief to him to find that in a

minute or two the train was running faster than ever, the driver no doubt wishing to make up for lost time.

Brandon carefully turned back her skirt, and the fine linen petticoats underneath it, exposing to view a pair of well-shaped legs encased in black silk stockings, and encircled by very natty-looking garters with red bows. Just above each of these garters was a frill of that lace which ladies call "insertion" — probably because the sight of it, in that particular place, so often leads to insertions of another kind.

Pulling apart her thighs as gently as though he were touching a sleeping child, he saw with pleasure that the slit of her drawers was a large one. The charms he sought were, however, hidden from his eyes by a chemise of the finest cambric. Carefully lifting this, he saw before his entranced eyes, now gleaming with lust, a forest of golden brown curly hair which extended, in a triangular shape from the line where the thighs join the body, all over the lower part of the belly. At the apex of this triangle, there peered through a thicker and curlier tuft of hair the pouting red lips of a pretty and very tempting looking abode of love.

To a man in the condition in which Brandon then was, this sight would have aroused all his sexual passions; uttering an exclamation of joy, he tore open his trousers, and there sprang out, ready for the fray, his huge member rearing aloft at the end of the big, straight hard column of muscle the round red gland which had hunted love through so many soft, damp, velvety caverns, and though exhausted by the chase, was ever ready to begin again after a short rest. At that moment the lady opened her eyes, and the first thing she caught sight of was the big machine prepared to impale her. Now if Mrs Sinclair had, as she was at first inclined to do, consented to having a little "flutter" with Brandon, she would have been extremely pleased with the fine proportions of the member that was to give her the pleasure she anticipated. But, however much a woman may like that amusement which a novelist has defined as being "the best game for two," she always makes her preliminary consent a *sine qua non*, and has a very decided objection to being forced. This is not unnatural, for if we received a man as a guest, and gave him a good dinner, and all that he could desire before he went away, we should certainly feel aggrieved if he came back in the night and tried to effect a burglarious entrance.

Mrs Sinclair therefore did what any woman would have done under similar circumstances — she gave a little gasping cry, and tried to get up, but as Brandon was then kneeling between her legs, and just in the act of lowering his dart to the level of her love nest, she could not, of course, rise.

The painter had his eyes fixed on the haven for which he lusted, and was not aware until he felt her move that she had returned to consciousness. He at once realized that he had spoiled all chance of "having" her by her own free consent, and that the only thing to be done was to rape her. He instantly threw himself upon her, and by his sheer weight pinned her down to the seat. With his right hand he tried to cover her mouth and so prevent her screams, whilst with his left he grasped hold of his yard and endeavoured to direct it into her slit.

This was no easy matter, for she wriggled her buttocks about so furiously that it was impossible for him to effect an entrance. She struggled with all her might, and bit Brandon's hand till the blood came, but, fortunately for him his weight pressed nearly all the wind out of the little woman, and the loudest scream she could give was not heard amidst the rattle and din of the train that was flying at sixty miles an hour.

Mad with lust, he kept driving his powerful tool against her, bruising her thighs, the lips of her coynte, and her perineum, and once or twice as she squirmed about, the big head of Brandon's member came very near inserting itself in a hole that was certainly never intended to receive it.

Worn out and exhausted by her struggles, she at last lay panting and motionless, and Brandon took advantage of that, and slipping his right hand down, he opened the lips of her love-cleft with his left hand, whilst with the right he directed the head of his member in the way it should go, and lodged it in her.

As soon as she felt this, she gave a start that nearly dislodged him, and began another series of frantic wrigglings, one of which had the very reverse effect to what was intended, for as she arched up her buttocks that she might better be able to twist sideways and get rid of the intruder, Brandon gave a powerful downward lunge, and as the head of his tool was already within her lips, the double force sent two thirds of his big column into her vulva.

She knew then that he had won the game, and woman-like, burst into a flood of tears.

This would have disconcerted Brandon at any other time, but as the old proverb says, "a standing cock has no conscience," and his only reply to her tears was to grasp one of her buttocks with each hand, and give a drive which sent his member up to the very hilt in her coynte. He had only just done so when his excitement, and the time he had lost in getting in produced their effect, and he poured into her vagina the warm flood which she would have been so glad to receive and mingle with her own love fountain, if the tool which was shooting the warm jets into her had come as a friend and not as an enemy.

A few seconds later and that enemy hung limp and diminished to a third of its size, and the two pink lips now indeed bright red, partly from indignation and partly from friction — had closed against the robber the Paradise into which he would have liked to intrude again.

Brandon slipped off her, and hastily buttoned up his "fly," keeping an eyes on the lady meanwhile to see that she did not jump up and make a dash for the "alarm," but she was two broken-down, weak, and, ashamed for any act of that sort. She could only cover her face with her hands and sob hysterically.

Brandon, now that the excitement was over, was very much ashamed of himself. He felt that he had not only deprived himself of any chance of ever winning her love, but he had by committing a crime upon her, put himself at her mercy, and that it was in her power to send him to the hulks. Even if she did not, and was willing to forgive him, he knew that he had acted like a blackguard and felt little inclined to forgive himself, and as he looked down on the pretty, little woman lying there with her clothing still disarranged, he felt very much inclined to pick up the little revolver still lying on the floor, and shoot himself.

She continued to sob convulsively, and Brandon after arranging her dress, and covering up the traces of his misdeed, knelt down on the floor by her side and tried to comfort her, for like most men, he was not proof against a pretty woman's tears.

"Go away!" she sobbed through her fingers. "You are a bad, wicked man, and I hate you! What would my husband think if he knew it? He would kill me, and you too."

"Yes, I know I am an awful scoundrel," said Brandon apologetically, "but you will forgive me, darling, will you not? It was not my fault; but you looked so beautiful as you lay in my arms that I could not resist the temptation. It was very wrong of me I own, but I was carried away by my love. It was your fault too, you know," he continued. "What man could be alone with the prettiest and most lovable woman in the world and not burn to possess her? It was not possible that I should not love you. Here!" he cried as he picked up the little revolver from the ground and held it towards her. "Punish me as I deserve. Death from your sweet hand would be delightful, and I should die with your memory in my heart."

Few women are not open to flattery and Brandon's admiration was so evidently genuine that Mrs Sinclair — for that was the lady's name — was touched. She began to reflect that though she had been cruelly wronged, the harm was not so very great after all. She was a married woman, and it was not the first time that a man's tool had visited her pretty little pouting coynte, and she had not therefore the loss of her virginity to deplore.

Besides, there were two other reasons which helped to make her inclined to pardon her ravisher. In the first place her conscience told her that she had rather encouraged Brandon, and that she had been on the point of freely giving him that which he had so roughly taken. Moreover she was of an ardent and amorous temperament, and though she loved her husband dearly, he was in delicate health and but rarely performed the act of love, and when he did, he was but poorly furnished, and his tool which was thin and short, had never penetrated to the bottom of her vagina. Her coynte still tingled from the friction occasioned by Brandon's long and vigorous shoves, and was considerably stretched by the huge engine that had so ruthlessly buried its whole length in her, but now the painful burning sensation caused by the forcible intromission had passed away, she felt a kind of pride and satisfaction to think that she had been able to accommodate in her little slit a huge tool which would have satisfied the most exacting and lustful.

She therefore pushed away the proffered revolver.

"No, no," she said, "there has been mischief enough already. Because you have committed a crime it does not follow that I should commit a worse one."

"Well then," cried Brandon, pointing the revolver at his own head, "tell me you forgive me, or I will punish myself for having wronged the most beautiful and most adorable of women."

She quickly caught hold of his hand, and wrested the revolver from his grasp.

"Yes, yes! I forgive you," she murmured, blushing; "you have been very cruel and unkind, and you have hurt me very much — but it was partly my fault. I let you talk to me when I ought to have stopped you at once and, and — I know you take me for a loose woman — and — oh, I am so miserable," and she began to sob.

"No, no," cried Brandon; "how could I think so, my darling. I am a brute, and my brutish passions got the better of me, but you are a pure, little angel."

She smiled feebly through her tears, and he kissed her, but she pushed him away.

"I forgive you," she said, "but I can't like you. I believe you have broken everything I have got. I am so ill, and I am quite sore. I believe I shall die."

"Oh, no," said Brandon with a laugh, "ladies can take a lot of that sort of killing. You will soon be better." He opened his hand-bag, took out a pocket-flask, and poured out some brandy and water. "Take a sip of this," he said, "and you will be all right."

She sat up, took the cup, and drank a mouthful or two. Suddenly a thought flashed across her mind.

"Oh, if the train were to stop now," she said, "and people saw me like this. Everybody would know what had happened, and I should be ruined. Quickly help me to dress."

She began to hastily smooth down her petticoats, and then going to her hand-bag she took out a comb and a hand-mirror, and began to arrange her hair.

She completed this to her satisfaction, adjusted her hat, and took a final look at herself. Brandon watched her admiringly, and would have liked to untidy her again, long before she had completed the process.

"I don't look very pretty," she said, more to herself

than to him, "my eyes are all swollen with crying. The next time we stop perhaps, I shall have time to go to the lady's waiting-room and have a wash."

"And of course you would not come back again," said Brandon rather bitterly.

"Of course I should," she retorted quickly. "That is just like you men — you always go by what you think yourselves, and not what other people *would* think. If I were to change carriages now, the guard would know at once that I had some reason for leaving your company, and very likely tell lots of other people his suspicions. Whereas if I come back he will not know" — this with a sigh — "that I have any reason to complain of your conduct towards me."

"You are a clever little woman," he replied. "I should never have thought of that."

He tried to take her hand and kiss it, but she drew it away hastily.

"There is one thing you must promise me faithfully," she said quickly. "I only consent to make the rest of the journey with you for the purpose of saving my reputation, but you, on your part, must give me your word of honour as a gentleman that you will not touch me, or, even speak to me unless I give you permission. Considering the outrageous nature of your conduct towards me you cannot very well refuse, if you expect me to overlook your bad behaviour."

"It is a hard thing to ask," he replied dolefully, "and I can only hope that you will give me the permission of which you speak; but I am bound to obey your wishes."

She bowed coldly, and did not speak, but retired to the corner in which she had at first been seated, and throwing her cloak over her, so as to hide her face, remained silent and motionless.

Brandon for his part sat in his own corner and tried to sleep, but the little figure before him, hidden under the Scotch plaid, prevented him from closing his eyes.

He was one of those fortunate men who are known amongst women of pleasure as a "revolver," and he would have loved to recommence the combat under changed conditions, for he was in hopes that before the long journey was over she would consent to give him freely the second time that which he had been obliged to take by force on the first occasion. He had, however, given his word, and was resolved not to break it, so he lay back in his corner and tried to doze, but he was not sorry when, half an hour later, the train slackened speed and then drew up at a large station.

AN UNDESERVED
PUNISHMENT

THE BUTTOCKS PAY FOR THE
COYNTE'S MISDEEDS

THE train had hardly come to a standstill, before the guard had jumped out of his van, and was running down the platform. "Ten minutes here," he cried.

When he arrived at the compartment in which Brandon and Mrs Sinclair were seated, he opened the door quickly and took a glance round.

"Ten minutes for refreshment, sir," he said addressing Brandon.

Mrs Sinclair rose from her seat, walked to the door, and the guard helped her out. She was still very sore from the severe doing she had had, and the guard, who guessed well enough the reason of her tottering walk, watched her out of the corner of his eye. He slightly shrugged his shoulders, and passed on to the next compartment.

When he arrived at the last compartment, he opened the door and saw four gentlemen sitting there, one in each corner.

"You have ten minutes here, gentlemen," he said, "if you like to get out."

"Oh, we're all right," growled a giant who was sitting in the corner next the door. "We've got all we want except a bedfellow — the Company ought to provide nice girls for the use of first-class passengers."

The guard laughed.

"There's a gentleman in the last compartment found one for himself," he said. "I should say she's had a rare good poking, if one may judge by the look of her."

"What sort of a tart is she?" asked a voice from the distant corner.

"Oh, you'll see her come out of the ladies' waiting-room in a minute," the guard answered carelessly. "I expect she's gone to get a wash, and I reckon she wants it," and he walked away.

A minute or two later, Mrs Sinclair appeared on the platform, and walked towards the carriage door which Brandon immediately opened for her.

"By Jove!" said the giant, and gave a low whistle.

"What's the matter, old man?" asked one of his companions.

"Why it's my brother Ted's wife," said the giant. "I didn't think she was likely to play the whore, but all women are alike. Let's change carriages boys; she shan't have another opportunity to get rogered before she reaches Glasgow, if I can help it; come along you fellows;" and he picked up his hand-bag, and a long roll in which an umbrella and two or three walking-sticks were packed up with a railway rug, and hastily descended.

The others grumbled a good deal, but they descended, and followed the giant, who stepped into the compartment in which Brandon and Mrs Sinclair were sitting, and was quickly followed by the others.

Brandon resigned himself to this incursion. On thinking the matter over he had come to the conclusion that it was more than improbable that Mrs Sinclair would invite him, or even permit, him to roger her a second time, and the idea of raping a woman twice in the same night was, of course, out of the question. He was not therefore much annoyed at seeing the carriage invaded by four men, indeed he thought it would give him an opportunity for a conversation with the lady.

Mrs Sinclair for her part had snuggled down into the corner, and with a plaid over her face, pretended to be asleep, or to be trying to go to sleep.

In another minute the guard came along and shut the doors. He looked rather surprised to see that the four men had changed their quarters, but, after all, they were free to do so if they chose, and it was no concern of his, so he sounded his whistle, and the train moved slowly out of the station.

The four men were seated together at one end of the carriage, and as soon as the train quickened its speed they bent forward, put their heads close together, and began to whisper. The big man, who appeared to be the leader, glanced several times at the lady, and once or twice at Brandon. At last they seemed to have come to some conclusion to which they all agreed, and after a great deal of acquiescive nodding of their heads, they resumed their upright position, three of them keeping their eyes fixed on the leader, who after a short pause, said in a loud voice:

"Have I not the pleasure of addressing Mrs Edward Sinclair?"

The lady started, and removing the shawl that was over her face, looked at the speaker.

"Oh, how do you do!" she replied. "I had no idea that my brother-in-law was in the train."

"*I'm* all right," replied the big man with a singular accent on the first word. "How is Ted, and why is he not with you?"

"His health is not very good," replied the lady, "so that I was obliged to come to town by myself."

"But you are not going back by yourself," said the big man jovially, "this is your brother I suppose," and he looked at Brandon.

The painter lowered his eyes, and the lady blushed scarlet.

"No!" she stammered, "this gentleman is a stranger to me."

"Oh, indeed," said the giant in a singular tone of voice. He made a few more commonplace remarks, and then the conversation died out; the lady once more settled herself in her corner.

The four men again put their heads together, and held a whispered colloquy. Brandon noticed that they several times glanced at him, and he heard occasional fragments of the conversation which puzzled him, such, as "No earthly doubt about it." "Secure him first." "A strap or a stick, or both?" "She shall get it hot;" but he eventually closed his eyes and went fast asleep.

⁂

He woke up with a violent start from a nightmare, in which he had dreamed that a horrible monster, half snake, half dragon, had seized him in its coils, and found himself firmly gripped in the giant's huge hands. Even in a fair struggle, Brandon, though a fairly strong man, would have been no match for the Herculean Scot, but taken unawares as he was, he could not make a struggle, and almost before he knew what had occurred, his arms had been forced backwards, and a thick oak stick passed under his two elbows. His arms and legs were further secured by a couple of straps, and he was quite helpless.

"We don't intend to hurt you," said the giant, "and all you have to do is to keep quiet. Now then, Sinclair, wake up!" he continued in a loud voice. "I have a question or two to put to you, and I hope you will answer them."

The lady, who had really been fast asleep, started and looked round her in a dazed sort of way.

"What is the matter?" she asked.

"Oh, perhaps there is a good deal the matter," replied the big man with a grin, "but what I want to know first and foremost is whether this man here has poked you in the train?"

"Sir," cried Mrs Sinclair, "how dare you insult me. What right have you to put such an abominable question to me?

"My brother is not here to protect his own honour, so I shall protect it for him," was the reply. "And let me remark that you have not yet answered the question. Has this man poked you or not? Yes or no?"

After attempting one or two more subterfuges, Mrs Sinclair burst forth with:

"Well, if you wish to know the truth, that man made an indecent assault upon me; in fact raped me."

"A very likely story," said the big man with a sneer. "You could have pulled the alarm signal, and stopped the train."

"But I had fainted," said the lady.

"Well, at any rate you could have complained when we stopped just now, and given your assailant in charge, instead of which you actually got out of the carriage and then returned — a pretty evident proof that you expected and hoped to get another poke before you reached Glasgow."

Mrs Sinclair was silent. She was ashamed to confess the truth, and was, more, pretty sure that she would not be believed if she did. Brandon tried to come to her assistance and assured the big man that she had told the truth.

"Oh, of course you would bear her out in anything she said," retorted the giant. "If you did commit a rape you deserve to have your balls cut out, but it is evident to me that you poked her, and she let you do it, and that you hoped to poke her again.

"As for you," he added, turning to Mrs Sinclair, "it is evident you have betrayed your husband's honour. I do not propose to make a scandal which would end in the Divorce Court, or even to tell my brother anything about it for he is a poor weak sort of chap, very different from me, and it would perhaps break his heart. But I cannot allow you to play the whore and not suffer for it, and so I and my friends intend to give you a good flogging on your bare bottom — one that you will not forget in a hurry, and that you will feel all the more because it is administered in the presence of your paramour."

It may be as well to make a short digression here for the purpose of explaining who this man was. He belonged to a self-constituted Society of National Purity, which, as the sequel will show, rather helped to spread unclean practices and create impure thoughts; as for the rest, is the natural tendency of all such associations. These men sometimes took upon themselves to apply the necessary correction, or antidote, and the world at large would be indeed startled did it know of the impure punishments inflicted in its name and for its social purification. Now and again the radical newspapers hinted at their goings on, and occasionally a prosecution would result, but this nefarious gang still exists to rape our girls under pretence of saving their virtue; violate our wives the better to preserve their chastity; and batten on the bodies of the outcast in order to satisfy their own lusts when occasion offered. We give an account of the latest member of this gang brought to justice, the prisoner having been one of the chief acolytes of Mrs Sinclair's brother-in-law.

THE MASSAGE SCANDAL

HYPOCRITE AND BLACKMAILER

AT the Old Bailey, before the Common Serjeant, George Francis Robertson, aged 27 years, described as a musician, was placed in the dock to answer a charge of having demanded money with menaces from Janette Aspeaslagh. There were two other charges of demanding money with menace from two other young women. Mr J. R. Randolph, who prosecuted, said if the evidence of the prosecutrix was true, the case was one of about as mean and as despicable a character as could well be imagined. The accused, who was a man of education and address, by vocation was a music-writer and known to several members of the Church of England. The allegations against him were that for some time past he had engaged himself on a pretended scheme for the suppression of massage establishments and houses of bad repute in the metropolis, in the course of which operation he had pursued a system of blackmailing of a heartless character. He called on Miss Aspeaslagh at St. John's Wood in October, and having paid her money, he subsequently demanded it back, saying that he was a "detective," and that unless she refunded the money he would lodge an information against the occupier of the house. As the result of the threat, the prosecutrix returned a sum of 10 s. which the prisoner had given her, although he had had carnal connection with this lady several times, he being a vigorous, very full-blooded man, so that she had been forced to cry out: "for God's sake not to split her in two."

Miss Aspeaslagh, a stylishly-dressed young woman with fine large breasts, hips like a Callipyge, roguish eyes and merry smile, described the visit which Robertson paid her, and said she was terrified by the prisoner into giving him his money back. Two letters were addressed to the National Vigilance Society by the prisoner. In one of these, Robertson, after referring to certain information which he said he had given to the police, went on to write:

"I am a little suspicious of the police and fear they may be guilty of bribery, and indeed often mount the girls and women they are supposed to suppress. I am delighted to think that there is a chance of something being done.... Madame M — is very artful, but anyone willing to spend a pound or more there can get any amount of beastliness and immorality; the girls will practice all the genital perversions known, such as flagellation, penis-sucking, etc. described in Dr Jacobus's *Ethnology of the Sixth Sense,* and *Genital Laws;* Madame herself being a "taker-on" and a whore of no mean capacity.... If I can help you I will, but I don't want to give evidence in court. Address me as follows: "Care of Rev. H. Mosley, M. A., Trinity Mission Club, Tenby-road, Stratford."

In a second letter, the prisoner wrote:

"All the printed matter sent by you is of great interest to me, and, though it reveals a terrible amount of Satanic dealings organized with persistency and skill, yet certainly the success of your work is matter for great thankfulness.... Your letter confirms my fears as to the practices universally carried on in the treatment for rheumatism, manicure, chiropody, etc.... I strongly suspect that women of shameless life are engaged in these practices."

The writer concluded the letter with a graphic description of a visit he paid to a massage establishment, where he saw ten naked women offering their various charms for all sorts of purposes, and enclosed papers which he said would show his good faith. He added that "Canon Scott Holland was a great friend of his."

A number of clergymen and other witnesses attended and gave the accused an excellent character, but the jury found him "Guilty."

Sergeant Croxton mentioned that there were similar cases against the accused, who would give information to the police, and then, learning that a warrant was out, go and attempt to get money from and operate on the bodies of the persons interested.

Mr Geoghegan said the prisoner's knowledge of Canon Scott Holland was merely in a business capacity.

The Common Serjeant said the one thing in the case

which made the conduct of the prisoner so odious was that he pretended to be carrying out a religious propaganda. That a man should be guilty of the conduct imputed to the prisoner, and indulge in religious exercises while fornicating and blackmailing like this, was a horrible revelation.

M[r] Geoghegan: He only writes music for religious journals. The prisoner instructs me that he never took any active part in the work of the mission. A man may perhaps appear a hypocrite to the external world and yet believe himself thoroughly conscientious.

The Common Serjeant: It is difficult to picture a more odious crime and the only redeeming feature is that prisoner has not gone into the witness-box and perjured himself, as was now so common a practice. I have no doubt that the prisoner has been carrying on this nefarious and abominable traffic in going to these houses and indulging himself in immorality and then demanding money from unfortunate women, for some time past. The prisoner was sentenced to four year's penal servitude.

Let us now return to the excited group in the train, where in a first-class compartment of the "Flying Scotchman," a refined lady is to be unjustly and shamefully beaten by, and in the presence of, strange men.

Little had she dreamt, poor woman, in boarding the train at Euston, that in the space of a few hours she was first to be forcibly ravished, and experience pleasure in the ravishment even against her own will, and finally have her silk dresses and petticoats tucked up, her linen torn, and she, a lady of education and position, held down by rough firm hands while her naked elegant, plump, white-velvet, beautifully rounded backside was exposed to the fury of a merciless whipping. Fate has indeed bizarre surprises in store for many of us, surpassing the ravings of poets, or the unreal dreams of neurotic novelists.

At a signal from the spokesman, the other men seized hold of Mrs Sinclair by the arms, and despite her struggles, laid her face downwards upon the seat of the compartment.

She seemed like a mere child in their grasp and with a few rapid movements, to which they were evidently accustomed, they soon had the struggling woman helplessly fastened with silk handkerchiefs bound round her wrists and arms.

But her legs were still free and she used them to very good purpose, for already one of the men had received such a kick in his balls that we warrant he must not have been able to have rogered his wife for at least eighteen months afterwards. He simply howled with pain, and was about to strike the woman a blow when he stopped suddenly short at a look from his leader, who muttered between his teeth: "The whorish bitch shall pay you back for that with her arse."

She screamed loudly for help, and kicked and struggled in a most desperate way, but these gentlemen were evidently thoroughly habituated to such scenes, for their eyes sparkled with delight and their lips wore a grim smile of enjoyment while they tried to master the terrified woman.

Never again, we undertake to say, would a railway compartment be destined to witness such a glorious picture of white buttocks, and voluptuous female flesh writhing and twisting and struggling in a most outrageous fashion to hide themselves from the view of these prurient male eyes which seemed to gloat over the helplessness of their intended victim.

Which of the gods is like thee, our queen?
Venus Callipyge, nameless, nude,
Thou with the knowledge of all indued

Secrets of life and the dreams that mean
Loves that are not, as are mortals', hued
All rose and lily, but linger unseen
Passion-flowers purpled, garlands of green!

Who like thyself shall command our ways?
Who has such pleasures and pain for hire?
Who can awake such a mortal fire
In the veins of a man, that deathly days
Have robbed of the masteries of desire?
Who can give garlands of fadeless bays
Unto the sorrow and pain we praise?

After a few moments, the leader made sign to his acolytes, who immediately began very carefully and slowly to draw back the panting woman's dress, which they folded back as far as her waist. Then they served a stout travelling flannel petticoat in the same way, and also a rose-coloured silk petticoat that she wore next to her drawers.

This latter article of feminine toilette calls for special remark. There is great psychological significance in the quality of woman's drawers. We firmly believe, with the talented author of an extraordinary book, which in itself is a perfect exposition of the philosophy of female discipline, — that the tightness or roominess of ladies' drawers exercises inevitably a most powerful influence upon their sexual desires and morals.

We take the liberty of digressing for a moment to quote a passage from that classic of flagellation literature: *The Mysteries of Verbena House, or Miss Bellasis Birched for Thieving*, attributed to George Augustus Sala, who is said to have been a most notorious flagellator. A passage which should be written out in letters of gold and hung up in the chief room of every thorough-going English family:

"The greatest enemy of woman's chastity is contact. Let her wear her things loose and she may keep her blood cool. Nuns — continental ones at least — don't wear drawers. Peasant women, who are chaste enough as times go, don't wear drawers; and when they stoop you may see the bare flesh of their thighs above their ungartered stockings. But the bigger the whore — professional or otherwise — the nicer will be the drawers she wears, while the prude, or the cantankerous old maid will either wear the most hideous breeches imaginable, or none at all. I positively knew a lady once who not only repudiated drawers herself, but would not allow her daughters to wear them."

The drawers worn by Mrs Sinclair were of the finest cambric texture, fringed and most beautifully embroidered.

They seemed to cling to her skin with the caress of a man's hand, and were quite warm from the contact of her body. They were what we should call "indecent" drawers, for they could not have failed to give birth in the bosom — and something else — of their charming wearer to most voluptuous feelings.

At a further sign of the leader, one of the men produced a pair of scissors, and proceeded ruthlessly to cut away the strings and tapes that bound them. The second subordinate then tore them off, and exposed her naked bottom, laying bare the most wonderful riches that it has ever been the lot of man to gaze upon. For such a sight the Turkish Sultan would have given all the treasures of his palace, and an American nabob would have bartered all the auriferous Mines of Klondyke for one view through the carriage window.

But the train still tore on its mad, headlong course, and the Turkish Sultan slept between the thighs of his favourite odalisque, little dreaming of such a scene as this. Her buttocks, though rather small, were exquisitely shaped, and the flesh was firm, and beautifully white, and smooth. Angry and helpless as Brandon was at the thought that he could not help his mistress, he was struck by her charms, and despite himself, his tool stood stiffly, and he could not help confessing that if he would have liked to have birched that pretty little bottom it would only have been to a sufficient degree to give a higher zest to the delicious poking which would have followed.

She blushed scarlet when she found her body exposed to the gaze of five men, and the blush suffused her whole body making her well-rounded buttocks flush a rosy red.

"Shall we gag her?" asked one of the men.

"I should like to enjoy her screams," replied the big man, "and then should know for certain she was feeling her punishment, but I suppose it is better to be on the safe side, so you had better gag her in case her screams should be heard."

The third man quickly tied a handkerchief loosely over her mouth, leaving her nose free, in order that she might breathe.

"It is a pity we have not a birch rod," said her brother-in-law, "we could have tickled up her arse in fine style, but I suppose we shall have to give her the strap."

"You will find a nice pliable cane amongst my sticks and umbrellas," said one of the men. "Here, up in the rack."

The giant went to the place indicated, and found a long thin pliable cane, which he swished in the air half-a-dozen times.

"Yes, this will make the little bitch jump," he said, "but I will prepare the way for it by first giving her a dozen with the strap."

He twirled the strap in the air, and brought it down with a dexterous sharp jerk across her buttocks diagonally from the left flank to the right thigh. A bright red band marked the expanse of white.

Shifting his position slightly, he brought down the strap again and this time it was followed by a red mark which crossed the bottom in the other direction.

"By Jove!" said one of the men who was holding her down, "you have marked her bottom with St. Andrew's Cross."

"And now it looks something like the Union Jack," said Sinclair, as he brought down the strap straight across both cheeks of her arse.

The woman had borne the pain pretty well. Though her pretty bottom was bright red all over long before the twelfth blow had fallen, the pain though severe was not intolerable, and she only moaned and sobbed, more with the thought that her naked person was exposed to the lustful gaze of so many men rather than from the physical pain she suffered.

"The tawse doesn't seem to have hurt her much," said one of the men.

"No, but it has made her nice and tender for the cane," replied the big man. "You had better handle that, Jock, and I will take your place and hold her down. I am a bit too heavy-handed, and I might hurt her too much — besides you are a schoolmaster and ought to know how to apply a cane properly."

"You bet I do," said the man grimly. "You hold her, and I'll soon show you."

The two changed places, and the schoolmaster raising the cane above his shoulder, brought it down smartly with a quick motion of his forearm. Instantly a thin white line crossed the bright red buttocks, but it disappeared again and gave place to a livid weal.

The effect of the cut on Mrs Sinclair was remarkable. She uttered what would have been a piercing shriek if the handkerchief had not stopped it in a great measure, and her struggles were so great that the two strong men who were holding her were hardly able to keep her still.

Down came the cane again, and another weal marked her bottom, and the woman, in her vain efforts to shield her cruelly treated bottom, tried to turn over,

and despite the two men holding her, turned completely on her side. Rage and shame had made her
forget modesty, and she did not know that she was
displaying to the enraptured eyes of the men a large
triangular fleece of golden chestnut hair, which
covered the whole of the lower part of her belly, and
beneath which could be seen the pink lips of her
dainty coynte.

Pretty as the spectacle was, the men quickly turned
her on her belly again, and down came the cane a
third time. There was another attempt at a scream;
through the handkerchief could be heard her voice in
a hoarse whisper, saying: "Oh, you wretches! Oh, you
curs! Oh, you beasts!" with even worse language which
would certainly have astonished her husband if he had
heard it.

The fourth, fifth, and sixth cuts descended on her
smarting bottom; and Mrs Sinclair arched her loins at
one moment and the next tried to press them into the
seat.

The man flogged slowly and methodically, allowing
time for each cut to have its full sting.

Seven! eight! nine! and the bottom, but a few
minutes before so dazzling white, was now a dull brick
red all over, crossed with livid seams.

The pain was intolerable and made the poor woman
scream out.

"Oh, don't!" she cried. "Oh! Ha! Ah! have mercy. Oh!
Oh! not so — hard — Oh! Oh! it will kill me. Oh! please
don't — I'm too soft — Oh! Oh! I shall die!"

None of the men took the slightest notice, and the
schoolmaster delivered the last three strokes as coolly
as though he had been beating his coat.

When he had finished, Mrs Sinclair lay huddled up
on the seat half swooning with pain. The men had
released her, but the sting of the cuts still remained,
and she continued to squirm and wriggle, at times
raising her body so much that the abode of love

between her legs could be plainly seen. Gradually the pain diminished and she was able to pull down her petticoats over her tortured bottom, and then she burst into a flood of tears.

The big man turned to Brandon.

"I was sorry to have to tie you up in this way, but there was no help for it," he said. "If you consider yourself aggrieved I will give you any satisfaction you like, but you had better hold your tongue. If you poked this woman with her consent she has been punished enough for her misdeeds and you would only ruin her reputation; whereas if you did rape her it might be unpleasant for you to have to do five years' hard labour. As it is we shall none of us say anything about tonight's work, and you had better follow our example."

With that they released Brandon, who in his rage and indignation would have attacked the men regardless of the odds against him, but at the sight of the shrinking and weeping figure in the corner, he remembered that a free fight would bring about a scandal, and that would cause the loss of her reputation, and he sunk back into his corner, moody and wrathful.

A few minutes later the train arrived at Edinburgh, and the men got out.

"What! changing carriages again, gentlemen?" cried the guard.

"Yes," said the big man, "we couldn't stand those love birds, and I hate to spoil sport, so we have determined to leave them alone — and here is a sovereign for you if you will do the same. Let them enjoy themselves as — as much as they can."

⁂

The vicinity of Glasgow is unmistakable. The flames of pauseless industries are here and there marked on the distance. Vast factories stand close to the track, and retching chimneys emit roseate flames. At last one may see upon a wall the strong reflection from furnaces, and against it the impish and inky figures of working men. A long, prison-like row of tenements, not at all resembling London, but in one way resembling New York, appeared to the left, and then sank out of sight like a phantom. At last the driver stopped the brave effort of his engine. The four hundred miles were come to the edge. The average speed of forty-nine and one-third miles each hour had been made, and it remained only to glide with the hauteur of a great express through the yard and into the station at Glasgow.

A wide and splendid collection of signal-lamps flowed toward the engine. With delicacy and care the train clanked over some switches, passed the signals, and then there shone a great blaze of arc-lamps, defining the wide sweep of the station roof. Smoothly, proudly, with all that vast dignity which had surrounded its exit from London, the express moved along its platform. It was the entrance into a gorgeous drawing-room of a man that was sure of everything. As the train definitely halted, a long, harsh gasp burst from the engine and a jet of white steam feathered overhead. A loud panting could be heard.

The porters and the people crowded forward. In their minds there may have floated dim images of the traditional music-halls, the bobbies, the 'buses, the 'Arrys and 'Arriets, the swells of London.

When they arrived at Glasgow, Mrs Sinclair allowed Brandon to lead her to a cab, for she could scarcely totter. He attempted to make profuse apologies to her for having been the cause of all her misfortunes, but she made a sign to him with her hand to be silent.

ACACIA VILLA, KELVINSIDE

BRANDON would have much liked to know the address of the pretty little woman to whom he had behaved so badly, but the gentlemanly instincts in his character re-asserted themselves, and he drew back when he saw Mrs Sinclair about to tell the driver the address, and taking off his hat made a low bow, and then stood and watched the cab out of sight.

The vehicle went off at a smart trot, and turning to the west, down one of the broad, straight streets which run parallel to the river, rounded the hill and stopped at a pretty little villa overlooking the Kelvin.

Mrs Sinclair had been obliged to sit as much as possible on one side, for each jolt of the cab was torture to her wealed and smarting bottom. She seemed so ill when she got out of the cab that the smart housemaid who had opened the front door and run down the garden to receive her mistress, looked quite frightened.

"I am rather tired, Jane; I will go straight to my room," said Mrs Sinclair, "and you can send me a cup of tea in half an hour."

She tottered across the hall, and with some difficulty ascended the stairs, and entered a pretty, little bedroom painted white and gold. She carefully locked the door, and then undressed with feverish haste. In a moment or two her dress and her snowy petticoats had fallen to the ground, and she stepped out of them. Then she undid her corsets, and released a pair of rather small but well-shaped breasts, the pink nipples of which peeped temptingly over the lace-trimmed hem of the chemise.

A few seconds later and she had removed her drawers, and then she slowly undid a button on each shoulder and the chemise glided off her white shoulders, and as it slipped down disclosed all the charms of her beautifully shaped form, her small and rounded waist, the fair white belly dimpled in its centre with a delightfully impudent looking navel, and below that the broad triangular forest of golden hair which but a few hours before had aroused the painter's lust, and below that the firm white columns of a pair of thighs, which, closed together as they were, concealed a sweeter charm than all, and tapered down to the black stockings on her shapely legs that set off the whiteness of her superb body, and made her look more undressed than though she had been really naked. If Brandon could but have seen her at that moment, he would have been strongly tempted to repeat his offence.

She stepped in front of a cheval-glass, and turning her head over her shoulder, looked sorrowfully at her scarred and wealed bottom, the scarlet hue of which contrasted so vividly with the rest of the delicate white body. Uttering a deep sigh, she walked to the dressing-table, and opening a pot of vaseline, gently applied it with her fingers to her smarting buttocks.

This relieved the smarting, and when she had dabbed on some violet-powder as well, she felt much less pain.

She took off her shoes and stood in all the naked beauty of her glorious womanhood, and pleased to be free from the painful pressure of her clothes, she walked about the room for a few minutes, and then stopped opposite to a framed photograph — the portrait of a good-looking but rather delicate young man.

"Ah, my poor Ted," she said as she looked at it. "If you had not gone to India and left your poor little wife at home, this would never have happened. And I do miss you so," she added, as she looked down at herself, and gently rolled one of the golden curls round her finger. "I believe that cruel beating only made you more excited," she went on, addressing her bower of bliss, "and that you would be glad if that big artist were to come in again now."

At that moment she heard the servant coming upstairs, and hastily slipping on her night-dress she unlocked the door, and got into bed.

The servant brought in the tea, and wished to stop and talk of all that had occurred during the absence of her mistress, but Mrs Sinclair quickly dismissed her, and having finished her cup of tea, lay on her side, and worn out by fatigue and the excitement of the adventures through which she had passed quickly fell asleep.

She did not wake till the following morning, and when she again examined herself in the cheval-glass she was pleased to find that the dull red colour had disappeared from her sacrificed bottom, which was now a bright pink, and that she felt hardly any pain, for the skin had not been broken. Mrs Sinclair did not leave the house all day, and the next morning she was nearly well, and by the third day no traces remained of the cruel treatment she had received.

Since her return she had received no visitors, for she feared lest some of the persons who were present might have told the story to others, and she dreaded lest her shame should be known.

She had occupied her leisure time in reading all sorts of books and papers. Cases of Rape seemed specially to attract her attention and to have over her mind a peculiar fascination. One evening after dinner, she was reclining on the sofa in the drawing-room when the following case caught her eye in the newspaper she was turning over:

SOLDIERS CHARGED

WITH OUTRAGING A YOUNG LADY

AT Scarborough, William McH..., private of the 1st York and Lancaster Regiment, and John William P...., gunner in the Royal Artillery, Scarborough Barracks, were charged with outraging Beatrice O...., aged 19, who resides at Gladstone Terrace, Bishop Street, Hull. The prosecutrix, who is a respectable-looking young lady, said that in company with her companion, Florence M...., she came from Hull to Scarborough on Saturday, with an excursion. On the South Sands the prisoners spoke to them, and offered to show them round the town. They told prisoners their train went at ten minutes to ten. Prisoners said they had plenty of time, but when they got to the station the train had gone. Prisoners then said they would find them lodgings for the night. They took them on the North Sands, and when prosecutrix protested that they could not get lodgings that way, the prisoner Palmer said they were to trust him. He had sisters of his own, and would see no wrong came to prosecutrix and her friend. At Scalby Mills Hotel they called up the landlord, but he said he could not accommodate them. It was now midnight. After leaving the hotel they went up the cliffs in the direction of the barracks. Prosecutrix heard her friend, who was with McH.., screaming, and asked Palmer what was the matter. Palmer, then said if she was not quiet he would throw her over the cliff top. Prosecutrix was terrified. Palmer next threw her on the ground, thrust one hand up her petticoats while, with the other he prevented her from rising and considerably hurt her breast. He parted her thighs and sought to ravish her. She struggled violently, screamed, and struck him in the face. Her clothing, was torn, her drawers were trailing on the ground and she wriggled about to her utmost, but despite her efforts, Palmer gained his purpose and succeeded in gaining complete intromission. Prosecutrix's friend, who had got away from McH.., then ran past screaming. McH.. followed, and seeing Palmer had prosecutrix on the ground, he stopped, and he also outraged her despite her struggles, his enormous member lacerating her genital parts so as to cause her great pain. Then they left her crying and exhausted. When she reached the town she found her companion complaining to Sergeant N. She related what had taken place, and was examined by Dr. H.

Prosecutrix's companion confirmed the statement. Both denied that they had more than a glass of port wine with the soldiers. The soldiers went into several public-houses, but they did not.

After Dr. H. had described the condition in which he found the girl, T.., a telegraph clerk, and the landlord of the Scalby Mills Hotel, who saw the parties, were both most emphatically of opinion that the men were quite sober.

Sergeant Normanton said that at half-past one in the morning he was in North Marine Road, when Florence M.... came to him. Her hat was on one side, her hair down, her jacket torn, and she seemed in great trouble, beads of perspiration being on her face. The prosecutrix then came up. She was in a very exhausted condition, and her tie and collar looked as if someone had had her by the throat. She looked as if she had had a desperate struggle and was holding a pair of white drawers (here produced) which appeared to have been torn.

Inspector B.... spoke to apprehending the prisoners at the Artillery Barracks. When he charged them they each replied, "I am not guilty," and followed on by stating: "We were with two girls at Scalby Mills, but we were so drunk that we don't know where we left them or what occurred."

Both prisoners said they were drunk, P.... adding: "Or it would not have occurred." Prisoners were committed to take their trial at the next York Assizes.

M[rs] Sinclair sat musing over this report and was wondering whether such shameful and intimate details would have been published about herself, had the affair in the train been proceeded with, when she was startled by a loud ring of the front-door bell and a moment later the servant appeared and announced, "M[r] John Sinclair." M[rs] Sinclair sprang to her feet, and was about to tell the servant not to admit him, but before she could do so he had entered the room, having closely followed the servant.

"All right, my dear little sister-in-law," he said in his rough coarse voice. "I was passing the door so I thought I would look in and see whether you had recovered from your — fatigue," and he laid a marked stress on the last word.

The poor woman sank back on the sofa, and threw a frightened glance at the intruder. She felt sure from his tone that if she ordered him out of the house, he would have no compunction in making public the story of her flogging, and that it would be impossible to stop the scandal that would follow. Her version would not be believed, and every one would think that she had deserved the punishment for her immoral conduct.

For John Sinclair had the reputation of being a highly respectable and most virtuous man. He was the "baillie" of a small country town, and was noted for being particularly down upon any unfortunate street-walker, and any poor girl who had listened to the voice of a seducer, and had in consequence to "let out" the seams of her dress, might indeed see her deceiver punished as heavily as the law would permit, but would herself receive such a lecture as she would never forget on the shocking depravity of her conduct.

He was also President of a Society for the Prevention of Vice — a society which ignored all the cardinal sins except that of lust — and he was connected with half a dozen Purity Societies and Societies for the Repeal of the Contagious Diseases Acts, and various other cheerful institutions of the same sort.

Mrs Sinclair, though she knew very little of him, as her husband had never greatly cared for his brother, had always mistrusted the man, and was of opinion that he was really no better than his neighbours, and indeed rather worse, because he was a hypocrite as well, but everybody believed that he really hated vice as much as he pretended to, and in Scotland he was looked upon as a pillar of morality, and quite a shining light to the nation at large. As a matter of fact, Mrs Sinclair's estimate of him was correct, and he was a monster of vice. Many a poor girl had he seduced, and one or two of them had ventured to accuse him publicly, but of course they were not believed, and their charges were held to be only malevolent perjuries.

The sight of his sister-in-law's bottom had aroused his lust, and ever since then he had brooded over the possibility of "having" his brother's wife, and the more he thought of it the more feasible it appeared, for it must be recollected that he really believed she had allowed the painter to roger her, and was unaware that she had been raped.

Being (as he imagined) inclined to be a whore, she would perhaps be disposed to favour a big strapping fellow such as he was, and though his conduct to her would hardly prepossess her in his favour, she would remember that he had it in his power to blast her good name, and would give from fear what she would not from affection.

He therefore boldly determined to pay a visit to her house, and as he shrewdly guessed that she might refuse to see him, he had, by the timely use of half-a-crown, prevailed on the servant to show him up at once.

At the sight of him, the recollection of the horrible punishment she had undergone at the hands of this detested man, flashed across M[rs] Sinclair's mind, and when she remembered that he had seen and felt her bare backside, she blushed scarlet, and with difficulty prevented herself from bursting into tears. He noticed her confusion, and thought he might turn it to good account.

"My dear Clara," he began — presuming on his relationship to address her by her Christian name, "I owe you an apology. The fact is, I was carried away by my feelings, for you know I have very strong opinions on morality. But I see now I was wrong. If my brother chooses to go away to India and leave a pretty little wife behind him, a widow in everything but name — it is but likely that her natural passions will break out now and then, and she will throw herself into the arms of the first good-looking fellow she meets."

"I do not understand you, sir," replied M[rs] Sinclair coldly. "You have intruded into my house in a most unwarrantable manner, and if I do not have you ejected it is only because I do not want to create a scandal, but I must beg that whilst you are here you will recollect who I am, and treat me with proper respect."

"Oh, yes," he replied with mock gravity, "and you might also treat me properly. You might remember that I am your husband's brother, and so like him that you might easily mistake me for him if you tried," — and he accompanied this sentence with a satyric leer.

"Sir!" cried M[rs] Sinclair. "It is very evident that you mean to insult me, and that you take me for one of those loose women whose society you frequent though all the world thinks you a very moral man."

"Well," he replied angrily, "if I am a hypocrite I am not the only one. You are not so overchaste when you are alone with a man in a railway carriage, and as we are both hypocrites, and both like to have a little bit of kypher when we can get it without anybody knowing about it, we might just as well enjoy a bit together;" and he leered at her again.

"I will not stay to be insulted," cried Mrs Sinclair. "You do not know the truth, or I cannot believe that you would make such unjust statements. It is true that the man who was in the carriage with me did have me as you would call it, but it was against my will and consent, and I made as much resistance to him as I possibly could."

"Even to the extent of pulling the alarm signal," said her brother-in-law with a grin.

"I was unable to do so," she replied, "but as I do not consider myself bound to account to you for my actions, I shall say no more."

"At all events you might have informed the guard when the train stopped."

"I am the best judge of my own actions," she said coldly, "and if I did not choose to make a scandal that is my affair."

He was silent for a moment, and then he rose from his chair, and held out his hand. She also rose, but did not attempt to take the proffered hand. He moved towards the door, and she followed him, but he suddenly turned, and catching her round the waist threw her on the sofa. She resisted desperately, but he was a powerfully-built man and he easily forced her down.

"You didn't mind being raped once, you little whore," he hissed through his teeth, "and so I don't see why you should mind it twice, at all events I mean to have you."

With one of his big hands he held her down, whilst

with the other he unbuttoned his trousers and pulled out a stiff standing tool of even larger proportions than that of the painter, and turning up her clothes, tried to separate her thighs which she pressed closely together. She did not scream, but she fought like a wild cat, and proved the truth of the saying that a man cannot put a sword in its sheath if the sheath keeps moving about. He did not start with the advantage that Brandon had, and great as his strength was he could not hold all her limbs at once and prevent her wriggling about.

Her underclothing was in a frightful state, the pink silk petticoat she had put on, being torn in several places, and her clean white drawers nearly wrenched from the strings that attached them to her waist.

The sight and odour of this underlinen seemed to madden the ravisher, whose pent-up unchastity now assumed absolute dominion over him. He resembled more a heat-maddened bull, or a stallion in rut, with his erect, flaming member thrusting vainly away at the panting creature in his grasp. And valiantly did she resist, with never a cry, fearing the shameful scandal should a servant appear.

"You filthy beast, let me go," she panted out in a hoarse whisper. "My husband will shoot you when he hears of this."

She wriggled and squirmed about like a snake, to get away, her shapely black-stockinged legs and prettily slippered feet high in the air and, kicking against the heavy table near by and which served as a lever for her efforts, she tried to push his member away with her hand, brushing against the thick mass of hair that surrounded his organs, as she did so.

"You bitch," he murmured, "let me put it in. No one will ever know. Good God! How I have longed for you! Have pity!"

But she broke away from him, taking advantage of his temporary sentimentality, and ran quickly round the table, making for the door at the far end of the room. He was too sharp for her however, and, his shirt front all crumpled, the collar torn, waistcoat and trousers disarranged, the organ still in a state of violent turgescence, his eyes bloodshot and half-starting out of his head, he managed again to seize hold of her just as she had put out her hand to pull open the door. With a blasphemous oath, he flung both arms around her, and struggling, kicking, turning, twisting, he bore her back to the sofa.

"Let me go, you fiend, I hate you!" she said. "Let me go or I'll tear out your eyes." But her strength was fast failing her, while determination to effect his purpose increased with her resistance, and made her only the more desirable. Already he had succeeded in putting one brawny knee between her thighs and with the other was furiously rubbing her genital parts; his face was pressed against hers and his hot breath scorched her like fire. She felt herself growing weaker, but the thought of this man's cruelty in the train — the terrible humiliation — the pain and exposure, gave her fresh strength.

The struggle had lasted long, but finally fate decided it in her favour. He had succeeded in forcing her legs well apart, and she was protecting her slit with both hands. As he tried to insert his huge member, it encountered her fingers, and she, with the energy of desperation, grasped it in her hand and exerting all her strength, bent it.

With a terrible cry, he staggered to an easy chair, and fell into it nearly fainting. She did not realize what she had done, and did not know till afterwards that she had dislocated his penis — a rare but exceedingly painful accident, the few instances of which that are known to have occurred having invariably ended fatally.

She saw at once that she had no longer anything to fear from him. He had fallen into an armchair, with his huge body drawn up, and was moaning.

Her first instinct was to run away and leave him, but she was a tender-hearted woman, and though he had twice made an assault upon her, she could not leave him in agony.

She went quickly to her bed-room, and as rapidly as she could, smoothed her hair, and did away with all traces of the struggle in which she had participated. Then snatching a coverlet from the bed, she went down to the drawing-room, and threw it over his legs, thus hiding the wounded member.

She then called one of the servants and sent her for a doctor who lived close by. The doctor was an old friend of hers, and when he came, she met him in the hall, and in a few words explained what had occurred.

He examined Mr Sinclair, and said he must be removed to the hospital at once, and calling his coachman they half led him, half carried him downstairs and placed him in the doctor's brougham.

At the hospital, they were unable to do anything for him except give injections of morphia to allay the intolerable pain. Several operations were tried by the Glasgow surgeons, who have the reputation of being amongst the cleverest in the world, but nothing was of any use, symptoms of gangrene soon manifested themselves, and in less than a week "holy Mr Sinclair" was dead.

In England, a false regard for Mother Grundy hushes them up, but we know of many cases which are highly instructive. For instance, the *Le Bien Public* (May 22, 1878) gave the following account of a trial before the Court of Assizes (Department of Var, France):

"The delicate operation that the learned Abeilard was forced to suffer at the hands of Canon Fulbert is a

well-known historical fact. Henri Latour, of Meones
(Var) has narrowly escaped becoming the victim of a
similar mutilation. This man had been acquainted for
about a year with a young orphan girl, Claire
Grimaud. She was a hard-working young girl. It was
not long before she perceived that she was in the
family way, and she informed her lover of it, who, she
affirms, thereupon promised to marry her.

"But, on the 29th of last December, in the evening,
Latour went to see Mlle Grimaud, whom he found
alone, when she remarked:

"You have come at last."

"The fact was he had been longer than usual
without coming to visit her. After conversing for a few
minutes they went to bed. The next morning, about
eleven o'clock, Latour felt his mistress getting up; but
she shortly came back, and again laid down by his
side, but without entering the bed. Latour wanted to
have connection with her; but he immediately
experienced a violent pain and found himself deluged
with blood. Nevertheless he had the strength to get up
and to go to a doctor, who gave him prompt
assistance.

"The medico-legal reports showed that the
unfortunate man had undergone an attempt at
castration, and it was for this crime that Claire
Grimaud appeared on this count before the Assizes.

"After the reading of the indictment, and at the
request of the prosecuting lawyer, the presiding judge
ordered the case to be heard with closed doors. The
public were only admitted at the judge's summing-up.
The female prisoner maintained that, until the
moment of her knowing Latour, her conduct had been
irreproachable. She had always been faithful to him
and had recently given birth to his child, a boy, while
in prison. It was owing to the refusal of her lover to
marry her and to recognize her child, that, she stated:
she gave way to a moment of indignation, which we

may add, the poor devil of a wooer, for his part, must have found uncommonly smart.

"The jury returned a verdict of not guilty on the counts presented to them, and the Court therefore pronounced the acquittal of the accused, who was immediately set at liberty.

"It is to be hoped however, that this sentence will not encourage other young ladies to follow the example given them by the passionate, penis-hacking Southern woman."

The fortitude displayed by some men who have received injury in their genital parts is simply amazing. Extenuating circumstances may, of course, be pleaded in those cases where honest steady women or girls are set upon by force, and attempts made to mount them against their will and consent. The man has then only to thank himself for all he gets. But if a woman invites a man to visit her and then, out of revenge strikes a blow, as dastardly as unexpected, at his copulative organs, she should be birched on the bare arse in public twenty times a year, suffer excision of the clitoris and made to undergo the operation of ovariotomy. We cite a further case, showing that truth is stranger than any fiction.

"On the 1st of December. 1836, the Court of Assize had to judge one of those crimes which are so rare that but a bare mention is made of them in article 316 of the French penal code, and of which the XIIth century has transmitted to us a celebrated and lamentable example. (3) But in this case it is not a man, but a young girl, who was able to conceive and to execute so atrocious a vengeance! It is not the jealousy of a rival, but the despair of an abandoned damsel, who came to resuscitate this sort of assassination forgotten by our new civilisation.

---

(3) *Héloïse and Abeilard.*

"Victoire Collet, of Thodure, attributed to Michel the paternity of two children to whom she had given birth, and Michel was seeking to contract other ties. After fruitless efforts to dissuade him from his purpose, Victoire, resigned to his marriage, was contented to ask for some pecuniary help. Michel, already affianced to another, and the banns about to be published, refused. Shortly afterwards he went to her place to claim some articles which she had taken possession of in order to oblige him to make her more frequent visits.

"He went there in the night of the 18th to 19th September, and the caresses of the discarded woman caused any misgivings of evil he may have harboured to vanish. Never had her reproaches been less bitter; Michel yielded. Victoire spoke of her legitimate fears of conception by reason of the already twice untimely results of their connection; and, when Michel, thinking of only sensual satisfaction, sought to press his favours home upon her, his mistress, armed with a knife, cut off his genital parts. Michel did not die from his wound within the next forty days. Victoire Collet who, at different times, had thrown out hints of her contemplated sinister vengeance, alleged in justification, that she had endeavoured to resist an attempt at rape.

"The argument presented to the Court, established pretty nearly the facts as related in the act of accusation, and revealed other intimate circumstances which made a deep impression upon the audience. The public was particularly affected when Michel being asked if he could not have taken hold of Victoire at the moment of her mutilating him, replied in a tone of the deepest emotion: *Ah! sir, if I could have caught hold of her, we should not be here!.... I perhaps, but she would not!*

"The prosecuting counsel maintained the indictment, not only with regard to the perpetration of the crime, but also as to its premeditation.

"M. Denantes, the defender of the accused, endeavoured to throw some interest on the case, by stigmatizing the cowardly abandonment by her seducer of this hot-blooded and revengeful female; and alleged in explanation and excuse for the crime the despair of the woman betrayed, and the anguish of the abandoned mother.

"He tried to invoke the protection of the legal-proviso offered in this case by article 325 of the penal code, to outraged modesty. Notwithstanding what the prosecuting counsel had said, he still alleged modesty of Victoire, in spite of her previous relations with Michel, the possibility of the outrage, and the right to resist it.

"With jesuistic quibble relative to the qualification of the offence, he maintained that there had been no physiological castration, therefore no castration in point of law. In fact, the mutilation does not interest the parts, the amputation of which constitutes castration. The crime imputed to Victoire must therefore be considered simply as cutting and wounding.

"The presiding judge summed up, the jury retired, and after an hour's deliberation, returned a verdict of guilty on the main issue, rejecting the plea of excuse, but admitting mitigating circumstances.

"The Court, on its part, maintained the qualification of the crime.

"In consequence thereof, Victoire Collet was sentenced, for the crime of castration, but with mitigating circumstances, to ten years' imprisonment."

A NYMPHOMANIAC

BRANDON watched the cab which conveyed Mrs Sinclair to her residence, until it had turned a corner and was out of sight. He had purposely drawn back when he heard her give her address to the cabman, for though he loved the little woman and bitterly repented his conduct towards her, he had resolved that he would not endeavour to make her acquaintance, unless accident or fortune should favour him in that respect.

When the cab had disappeared round the corner, Brandon picked up his portmanteau — for, being an experienced tourist he never overburdened himself with luggage — and started off at a swinging pace towards one of the suburbs.

At the end of an hour's walk, he stopped in front of a small villa, pushed open the gate, and entered the garden. In another moment, the front door was thrown open, and Maud came running down and threw herself into his arms.

He kissed her lovingly, for his conscience rather smote him when he remembered that he had been unfaithful to her a good many times during his absence, and had wound up with a criminal offence which might have led to his being locked up for some years.

She linked her arm through his, and they walked up the garden together. He turned and took a good look at her, and could not but be struck with the change in her appearance. She was untidily — almost shabbily

— dressed, which had never been the case even in their worst days of poverty, but it was in her face that he discerned the greatest change. Her eyes were sunken, and glittered with a strange brilliancy, and her face was preternaturally pale, with a red patch over each cheek-bone.

"You are not looking at all well, little woman," he said gravely. "Do you fell ill?"

She gave a strange little laugh, and cast down her eyes.

"Oh, I'm all right, I think," she answered; "but it has been very dull without you, and I missed you a good deal — especially at night;" she added, leaning against his side amorously, "but you will find I shall be all right to morrow morning if you are the same as you used to be, and have not left your heart with some pretty Swiss girl."

There was something in her tone more than her words, that vexed him.

"But you are looking very well, dear boy," she went on, "and that is enough for me. And now come along and have some dinner — I've got something you like."

She ran lightly into the house to see about his dinner, and he stood thoughtful.

It seem to him that there was an erotic meaning in all her words, and, however amorous a man may be, he seldom likes to find that in his wife, though he may in his mistress.

"I hope she has kept straight during my absence," he muttered to himself; "I was a fool to leave her by herself for so long, knowing what a hot nature she has."

Maud was very happy all day, and showed her husband many little attentions, and when they went to bed she proved that she had not forgotten her old habits: long before morning Brandon had to plead the fatigue of his journey as an excuse for not giving her as much as she wanted.

Before he had been at home many days, Brandon found there was a great change in his wife, and that she had become as she had been in the old days before his adventure with the French nobleman, except that she did not as then, care for dress, for she was now untidy and careless of her appearance. The only time when she seemed to care for him was when they were in bed together, and then if he did not feel inclined to give her what she wanted, she would turn sulky and bad tempered.

At last the conviction was fully brought home to his mind that his wife was becoming, if she had not already become, a confirmed nymphomane, caring for nothing but the carnal act. He was well aware that when once this disease attacks a woman, her moral degradation is only a question of time, for no man, however virile he may be, will be capable of supplying her sexual needs.

Nymphomaniacs, or in plain Anglo-Saxon: women love-mad, have existed in all ages, but do not appear to have engaged in a special manner the attention of the physicians of antiquity.

Hippocrates, Galen, Celsus, Areteus, Oribasius, and Paul of Ægina, who practised in Greece or in Italy, hardly make any mention of the existence of these passion-racked females; we must come down to Soranus, a Greek physician who practised and taught medicine in Rome towards the Third century, and had the highest reputation, and after him to Aetius, to find the earliest descriptions of the malady of the love-lost.

Attributed by Bonnet to the animal spirits inflamed by sensual love reacting upon the brain, upon the uterus, and upon the entire genital apparatus, this affection is now well known, and the description made of it with the greatest care and most scrupulous exactness proves that science has put an end to all of the more or less ingenious but erroneous theories of the ancient authors.

Contrary to what is observed in erotomania, the evil takes its rise in the organs of generation and it is only much later that the irritation acts upon the brain.

Although nymphomania, says Dr. Paul Moreau, is more frequently observed in subjects affected with mental alienation, it may nevertheless sometimes *show itself among women who have partly retained their intelligence and the conscience of their actions.*

Such cases, unfortunately, are not very rare, and there is nothing more sad, more heart-rending than to see woman a prey to the most hideous of maladies, carried away irresistibly, contrary to her will, fall lower in rank than a brute, and assist powerless at her own degradation.

In the course of a week or two he fancied also that he noticed a change in her figure, and this suspicion was soon confirmed — there could be no doubt about it, she was pregnant.

"Why Maud, I do believe you are in the family way," he said to her one day.

She started, and looked confused, and when she had recovered herself, replied:

"Yes, I fancy you must have made a baby just before you went away. I noticed that I was in for one just after you left."

"Oh, well," he said, good-humouredly. "I should like to have a child, and it is quite time we begun. In fact, I wonder why one or more have not come before."

Maud blushed scarlet and left the room quickly. Her manner struck Brandon as very peculiar, and a horrible suspicion which he was afraid to believe crossed his mind, but he resolved not to entertain it. Men are honester than women, an American novelist says, and his own conscience told him that if he knew his wife had been unfaithful to him, and the child now in her womb was not his, that he could hardly reproach her, for his own infidelities had been manifold. Yet man has been educated for centuries to

regard his own want of chastity as a mere trifle, or
indeed almost a necessity of his sexual nature, but for
a woman to fail to preserve her chastity he regards as
a most serious offence. It is true that this mental
attitude of his has been probably caused by the
women, for no one is so severe on the shortcomings of
an erring sister as your virtuous woman.

Some months went by, and though there were no
quarrels between Maud and her husband, there was
that constraint and reserve which is worse. For a good
quarrel will often clear the moral atmosphere, and as
the Latin poet said, lead to the renewal of love, but a
constant coolness is a damper on the affections.
Brandon often thought of the little woman he had met
in the train, and even made some slight efforts to
discover her whereabouts, but they were unsuccessful,
and Maud was so suspicious and jealous that he was
obliged to be circumspect.

The months went on, until one night, Maud, whose
belly was now very big, begged him to go and fetch the
doctor. He dressed at once, and hurried off to the
surgery, and in a few minutes had returned with the
medical man. Leaving him to attend to Maud, Brandon
hurried away to fetch the monthly nurse. It was a
bitterly cold November morning, with the snow falling
slightly, and the nurse lived in a distant part of the
city. Three o'clock had struck before he had reached
the nurse's lodging — it is curious that these affairs
usually occur during "the small hours beyond the
twelve" — and then of course there was the usual
delay whilst the nurse dressed and prepared that
mysterious parcel without which no follower of M^{rs}
Gamp who has a particle of self-respect would think of
moving a step.

Whilst he was waiting, Brandon could not help
thinking of the years that had elapsed since he
married Maud. He remembered the great love he bore
her, and how that love, though once crushed to earth,

had sprung up again, only to dwindle and slowly die out again. He confessed to himself that perhaps he had been to blame, for this latter part at least, and promised that when she recovered he would be a more affectionate husband, and by love and care, wean her from that moral depravity which was ruining her body and soul.

He was nervous and anxious during all the long ride home, and hardly heard the platitudes which the nurse uttered.

When he arrived home, the nurse at once hurried off to the bedroom where Maud was, and Brandon entered the dining room and sank into an easy chair. He mixed himself a stiff glass of whiskey and water — although as a rule he drank but little — and he tried to smoke to calm his nerves, but the occasional shrieks and moans which came from the bedroom, and which in the stillness of the night could be heard distinctly, sank into his soul, and he threw away the cigar, and swallowed the whiskey at a gulp without tasting it. There are few things which so upset a man's mind as the birth of his first child, but by the time he has a large family, his ear becomes "more Irish and less nice" besides there is not so much groaning and shrieking on the subsequent occasions.

He must have sat there a couple of hours, which seemed to him like a couple of centuries, when the door opened gently and the doctor appeared looking very grave.

"Is it all right?" asked Brandon in a hoarse whisper.

Being a medical man as well as a Scotsman there were two valid reasons why the doctor should not give a direct reply.

"It has been a most difficult and dangerous labour," he said — "perhaps the worst that I have ever met in all my practice."

"But it has ended satisfactorily, I hope," said Brandon in a choking voice.

"Mrs Brandon's habits of life," replied the doctor cautiously, "were not I should imagine conducive to an easy labour. It is a great pity she ever became pregnant."

"You are torturing me, doctor," cried Brandon, "tell me the worst, and I will try to bear it like a man."

"The child is dead," said the doctor gravely, "stillborn."

"And the mother?"

"We must do the best we can for her," said the doctor still more serious, "but I cannot conceal from you that she is in a very critical condition, and I cannot pronounce definitely yet whether she will recover. We must hope for the best."

"Can I see her?" murmured poor Brandon.

—"Yes — she wishes to see you, and I think it will be better that you should go to her — it may do her good."

With one bound Brandon was out of the door and half-way up the stairs. Then he stopped and tip-toed gently to the bed-room door, opened it, entered, and took a seat by the side of the bed.

A faint smile played over Maud's face. She looked extremely beautiful as she lay there, for all her old beauty had returned, and the wonderful masses of golden brown hair made her pale face seem wondrous fair.

"I am glad you have come," she whispered. "I wanted to see the baby and they won't show it to me."

Brandon glanced at the doctor, who had followed upstairs more slowly and was now standing by the side of the bed. The doctor made a sign of assent.

"The poor little thing is dead," her husband replied.

A look of pain came into her face, and she was silent for a minute. Then she looked at the doctor, and he, with professional quickness, caught her meaning. He made a sign to the nurse and they both withdrew to the other end of the room.

"I am glad of it," she whispered, "and I shall soon see it for I feel I am about to follow it."

"Don't say that, Maud; you will soon be better," replied her husband.

"I am glad it is dead," she repeated, "for I have been a bad wife, Bob, and the child was not yours. I'm too weak to tell you all, now; but say you forgive me and I shall die happy."

"I do forgive you, darling," said Brandon; "I have been more to blame than you."

He bent and kissed her fair face and she gently pressed his hand, and closed her eyes. The pressure gradually relaxed, and the doctor, who had been watching her closely, came to the bedside, took her hand and felt her pulse.

Soon he laid her hand down gently, walked round the bed, and touched Brandon on the shoulder.

"You had better come away, Mr Brandon," he said gently, "we can neither of us do any more good."

Robert Brandon was a widower.

IN THE TRANSVAAL

AFTER Maud's funeral the house seemed so dull and melancholy that Brandon hastened to sell off all the furniture. Life had become distasteful to him. He was alone in the world and had lost all interest in mundane affairs. He felt that if this continued he would be driven to suicide, and he had the sense to know that the only means to drive away these black thoughts was a thorough change of scene and surrounding.

He quickly got together all the money he could raise, and with three hundred pounds in his pocket started for Liverpool, resolved to take the first steamer — he neither knew nor cared whither.

He wandered round Liverpool docks, and seeing a large steamer about to start, asked whither it was bound, and learned that it was going to the Cape. He embarked, and reached Capetown without any incident or accident. In a few weeks he had nearly exhausted all his money, and was wondering what he should do next, when war between England and the Transvaal became almost certain.

His life still seemed dull and aimless, and though he had shaken off the suicidal thoughts he cared little to live, and it seemed to him that if some Boer's bullet should lay him low it would cause no grief to anyone, and be an honourable end to his own misery.

He lost no time in enlisting in one of the Cape regiments, and as he was a man of education, and had been a volunteer in England and knew something of soldiering he was quickly promoted to be sergeant.

In a few weeks war was declared, and it was with the utmost satisfaction that Brandon heard that his battalion was ordered to the front to join the forces under General Symons.

The officers of the Queen's troops found out quickly that he was a gentleman, and many of them had heard of him by reputation as an artist, so he soon became a general favourite amongst them, and more especially with a tall young, delicate looking man whose name was Captain Sinclair, and they used frequently to visit each other's tents.

Brandon soon discovered from his conversation and demeanour, that the Captain was no ordinary man. Of superior education, he was a profound thinker and had not Destiny made him a soldier it is clear that Nature would have turned him out a philosopher. Their talk was always of an intellectual kind and Brandon felt that he had met a man worth listening to on the rare occasions that his friend could be made to "let himself go," as he termed it. Once, when speaking of the marvellous power of the genital instinct, and of the magnetic influence that Woman exerted over Man, the Captain narrated the following remarkable dream, which struck Brandon so much that he made notes of it the same night on getting back to his own tent.

We give it as it was repeated to us.

CAPT. SINCLAIR'S DREAM

IT was in a tranquil space of immense extent, or else beneath the vast colonnades of a gigantic temple. I know not. It is the specialty of dreams to leave but indistinct notions which fade away, leaving to the awakening spirit only vague memories, so vague they can scarcely be defined.

A weird silence reigned around, strangely soft and

soothing to the soul... then hidden musicians, as if from the sky, breathed harmonious chords, in low, very low, soft tones. It was rather a murmur, a zephyr, than music.

Suddenly the tones rose higher and higher, until they abruptly ceased with a hoarse, fearful, piercing cry, a cry of horror, of disgust, of remorse, to give place to the crushing silence of anguish.

All at once the place was ablaze with light; thousands of lamps shone with a hard, dazzling glare. A pæan of triumphant pride arose, and the voice rather harsh, elevated and slightly shrill, sounded strangely in its mocking tones.

I then distinguished, seated on an elevated throne, draped in purple, the splendid body of a woman, absolutely perfect in form, and wearing over the deluge of dark luxuriant hair that served her for a mantle, a crown of diamonds so brilliant that they seemed like burning coals. Seated on the black fur of a bear, in an easy posture, she seemed very calm, stripping off the incessantly renewed petals of a daisy, her brilliant eyes lost in a far away dream, towards some invisible horizon, and her eyes of that limpid soft blue shade which seems to denote goodness, quietude and frankness.

Quite on the top of the very broad steps, lay extended, motionless, a man with the handsome body of an athlete, his eyes were fixed up above without bearing in them any expression of revolt or of hatred, but they were glassy, indicating clearly the void of an exhausted brain.

Upon his face the woman had placed her foot, without his making a movement, and for a moment remained fixed in her ecstatic attitude.

Then from below, there came another man who rushed up to her.

She tendered him her lips, then her body, and after tightly embracing her the man fell on the steps where he lay prostrate and crushed.

Two and three more came, and after them a crowd. There were magistrates, soldiers, peasants, workmen, rich and poor, young and old, from all countries, from each continent, and of all colours.

To each and every one she tendered her lips and abandoned her body, and they all fell down an inert mass...

And unceasingly the crowd increased. I saw the steps darkened by a howling mass of people rushing up, fighting to distance one another and arrive first.

There were cries, cries of wild beasts in heat when they rush towards the female, fighting for her; there were cries of suffering, cries of disgust, the heart-rending cries of those who, after possession saw nothing before them but void, absolute void.

The steps were crimsoned with the blood which trickled from the bodies.

Without ceasing, more and more compact, the crowd continued fighting... It was no longer a woman that offered herself, it was an incandescent body which burned all who approached it, but none of them were aware that they were burnt, and I understood that for all, here was the incarnation of supreme enjoyment, here was brought eternal desire, and that afterwards, all fell back with loathing and exhausted.

.　　.　　.　　.　　.　　.　　.　　.　　.

And while the multitude continued to fight, I saw close by, on a flowery mead, the athletes of Borh, who do not know the flesh, drinking Cyprus wine whilst they discuss the deathlessness of the soul.

✵

One night, Brandon feeling more than usually dull,

thought he would go and pay a call on the Captain.

He found the officer writing.

"Oh, I see you are busy," said Brandon, turning to go away.

"Oh no, come in," cried Captain Sinclair. "I have just finished a letter to my wife in Glasgow. We shall, I hear, have a brush with the enemy tomorrow, and as the Boers shoot straight, it is just as well to get my correspondence done beforehand."

"Glasgow!" repeated Brandon. "I did not know you came from Glasgow."

"Yes, I do. I have a charming little wife there, and a comfortable house, but I don't suppose I shall ever see them again. But as you are a Glasgie chiel let us have a talk over old times."

They talked till the bugle sounded "Lights out." Brandon had not mixed much in society, and knew but few of the Captains' friends, nor did it strike him that it was a Mrs Sinclair who had met with that strange adventure in the Scotch Express.

Early the next morning which was a Friday, all the troops were under arms to dislodge the Boers from their position on the mountain above Glencoe. (4)

The Boer plan of campaign was devised with considerable skill, and provided for a simultaneous attack upon Glencoe by three different columns aggregating about 7.000 men.

General Joubert's instructions to the commanders of the various columns were, it is understood,

---

(4) The scene of that Friday's great battle was a hill between Dundee and Glencoe. The Boer Artillery occupied the top of the hill. Their Artillery was silenced by ours, and then the hill was stormed by a gallant charge of the Dublin Fusiliers and the King's Royal Rifles. Our list of killed and wounded was estimated at 214. The Boers are said to have lost 800. The Boers approached Glencoe Camp from Landman's Drift, the border pass to the right of Dundee. Glencoe itself is on a high table land. It is forty-two miles N.W. of Ladysmith, where General White had a force of 9.000 strong.

distinctly to the effect that Erasmus was to lure the whole British forces on to the northern road towards Hattingspruit. While the British were engaged in the apparently easy task of wiping out Erasmus's column, Viljoen and Meyer were to fall upon them in rear and in flank and annihilate them.

Of all this General Symons was well aware, and he took his measures accordingly.

But the Boer plan of campaign came to grief. Being unable to keep in telegraphic touch with each other, the three commanders blundered on with no thought for the all-important question of time. The result was that Meyer's force precipitated the battle before even the Hattingspruit column was within striking distance, and while Viljoen and his Free Staters were a long way to the south. There was therefore no simultaneous attack and Meyer's force, numbering about 4.000 men, with six guns, had to bear the whole brunt of battle.

Not more than half our force advanced to the attack, for other dangers, believed to be imminent, had to be guarded against. The Boer column under Erasmus had been found by our scouts at Biggars drift to the south, only a few miles away, and the Hattingspruit contingent were reported to be moving from the north with the knowledge that the engagement had commenced without their indispensable co-operation. These two Columns would have brought the strength of the enemy up to 9.000 men. Therefore the 18th Hussars, the Leicester Regiment, the volunteers, and mounted infantry still remained in and near the camp.

Just before eight o'clock there came a diversion for our gunners. Hundreds of Boers were suddenly observed to be lining a hill to the west of the camp. They were the advanced detachments of the Hattingspruit column, but they had arrived on the scene too late to be of service to Lucas Meyer and his men. As soon as the new-comers came well into view, the 67th Battery, stationed behind the camp, opened fire upon them. Several shells burst amongst them. This was sufficient for the Hattingspruit contingent, which very speedily betook itself into a safer position out of reach of the terrible guns.

All this time, while the two batteries were pounding pitilessly at the Boers on Smith's Hill, the infantry were advancing steadily to close quarters with them. Three fine regiments were passing over the ground in almost faultless style — the Dublin Fusiliers, the King's Royal Rifles, and the Royal Irish Fusiliers. Encouraged by their officers, who too often belied their advice by their example, the men advanced in perfect order in skirmishing line, taking advantage of every bit of cover, halting only to fire by sections as they came within easy range of the enemy. For over an hour this steady advance continued, while the artillery gave the Boers not one moment's rest.

The Mounted Infantry were comfortably ensconced under the shelter of a large and thick plantation at the foot of the hill to the right, and just under Smith's Nek. The 18th Hussars had also moved out from the camp, and were working round the hill preparing a surprise for the Boers busily engaged in front.

In these positions all the men remained for a time, to take breath and prepare for the final onslaught upon the enemy. Then the advance was resumed over most trying and difficult ground. The critical moment had come.

The Boers poured down lead from Maxims and rifles, and, despite the clever manner in which our men took cover, they began to fall quickly.

By toilsome and steady work the Fusiliers and Riflemen at length secured good positions high up on the hillside, whence it would be feasible to make the final rush.

Suddenly the artillery ceased firing. Another moment, and at the word of command our men fired two volleys, and then with wild battle cries their pent-up emotion and energy found vent in an irresistible rush up the remainder of the hill, and a swinging charge right amongst the enemy. For a quarter of an hour there was bloody work at short range and then at close quarters. Then the Boers fled in disorderly retreat, closely pursed by our men and the Mounted Infantry.

As the enemy stampeded down the hillside they found to their dismay that the whole regiment of hussars had forestalled them. The cavalry had got right to the enemy's rear, had captured many of their horses, and stampeded the others. One contingent of the enemy were thus perfectly helpless. They fought well enough for a little time and then those who were left surrendered.

Parties of men were sent out to bring in the wounded and report the dead. Brandon was in one of these parties, and as he was examining the dead and wounded which lay thickly strewn in front of the Boer entrenchments, he fancied he heard his name whispered. He turned and saw, lying under a gigantic Boer, his friend Captain Sinclair.

With the assistance of a comrade, Brandon pulled away the huge corpse, but one glance at his friend showed him that he was seriously, if not mortally, wounded. Blood was slowly ebbing from a bullet wound in the breast, and he had also received a severe sabre cut from the gigantic Boer he had shot a moment later.

Brandon supported his friend's head, and told his comrade to run and fetch a litter if he could get one, in order to convey the wounded man to the field hospital.

"No, no," said Captain Sinclair, with more strength than could have been expected considering his condition; "I've got my billet, and no doctor can do me any good, so he had better not waste time over me. But you stay with me Brandon, for I feel I have not long to live, and I have a message I should like to send home." Brandon, of course, promised that he would perform any commissions the other charged him with.

"You will find in my tent," said the dying man, "a letter to my wife which I wrote last night. I had a presentiment I should get hit to-day, and I wrote my last wishes to her. Poor little woman, I shall never see her again in this world. I don't want you to post that letter to her. The war will soon be over, and then you will return to Scotland, no doubt, and I want you to see my wife and give her the letter. Tell her that I died blessing her name."

He paused a moment, exhausted, and Brandon gave him a sip of brandy.

"Tell her," continued Captain Sinclair, "that her portrait never left me till I placed it in your hands."

With an evidently painful effort, the dying man put his hand in his breast, and drew out a small leather case which he gave to Brandon. "Give her that, and the letter, with your own hands. Promise me that," he added eagerly.

"I promise you that, — if I live, — the portrait and letter shall be placed in your wife's hands.

The wounded man smiled gratefully, then a film came over his eyes, his head dropped back and he was dead.

A week later Brandon also received a bullet, but it was in his leg, and in a month he was on his feet again, but incapable of further active service, the bullet having injured one of the bones, so that he walked with a slight limp. This was not insufficient to incapacitate him for the cavalry, but so many regulars were arriving from England, that his services were declined by the military authorities.

He was not altogether sorry, for the excitement of the war had driven out of his mind the melancholy which had oppressed him, and he longed to see

England again. Besides he had promised to execute the dying wishes of Captain Sinclair.

He had found the letter in that officer's tent the day after the battle of Tulandand, and had put both letter and locket away in a safe place. The locket he had never opened, having been deterred from doing so by a feeling of delicacy or reverence for the dead man's wishes.

One of those lucky speculations which are only met with in half-civilized countries, had enabled him to make enough money to pay his passage and leave him a good bit over. He took passage in a Cape liner, and three weeks later was in Southampton; from thence he went to London, and the next night took his seat in the Scotch Express.

As he was borne along at the rate of sixty miles an hour, the memory of the last time he had undertaken the journey crossed his mind, and all the circumstance of that eventful night flashed before him.

"What a blackguard I was," he said to himself. "And how badly I behaved to that little woman. She could have put me in gaol for five years if she had liked, and I should have deserved it. I wonder who she was? I heard the big man call her some name that night, but I have clean forgotten what it was. I keep fancying it was Sinclair, but that of course is nonsense — a trick of the brain. By the way, I hope I shall know poor Sinclair's widow when I see her. I have never looked at her portrait yet — kept back by some indefinable feeling for the dead man — but as I am to see the lady in the flesh and blood within the next few hours, surely it can do no harm to look at her portrait."

He pulled the little case out of his pocket, opened it and stood up in order to get the full light of the lamp on it. As he looked, his eyes and mouth opened wide, and with a groan he dropped back in his seat.

"By Jove! the woman I raped in this very train!"

EPILOGUE

BRANDON'S first care on arriving at Glasgow was to disguise himself so effectually that there was no chance of recognizing him. Then he made his way to Acacia Villa, and told the servant that an old soldier, who had been with Captain Sinclair in Africa, wanted to see her mistress.

He was shown into the drawing-room, and in a few minutes Mrs Sinclair, looking very pretty in her widow's weeds, came into the room. Brandon, who had tried to make himself look like an old soldier, was glad to see she did not know him again. He told her all the particulars concerning her husband's death, and handed her the locket and the letter. She looked long at the locket with tears in her eyes, and she read the letter through carefully. As she reached the end she started and looked hard at Brandon. "Did my husband have brain fever, or sunstroke M^r...?"

"Thompson, mum. Bill Thompson — at your service," replied Brandon. "No, mum, I never see any signs of it."

Mrs Sinclair asked a few more questions, and when the messenger got up to leave she pressed a couple of sovereigns into his hand.

"I suppose an old soldier is not too proud to accept a present from an officer's widow," she said.

To her surprise the old soldier dropped on his knees before her.

"I can keep up this deceit no longer," he cried. "You

see before you the wretch who did you a cruel wrong, but who has never ceased to reproach himself for it. I loved you from the first moment I set eyes on you and the thought of you has been my stay in life many a weary night. Your image prevented me from taking my own life, or throwing it away, on a hundred occasions."

"Mr Brandon!" she gasped.

"Yes, madame," he replied, "the man who committed a dastardly offence on you; for which he again prays your forgiveness — and when he has attained that will dare to hope to win your love."

Mrs Sinclair was silent for a minute, then she handed her husband's letter to Brandon.

"Will you please read that paragraph?" she said.

Brandon took the paper and at the spot indicated read as follows:

"You are young, very pretty, innocent and confiding. If you are left alone and defenceless in the world, you will become the prey of the first swindler or scoundrel you come across. You are not the sort of woman who meant to cross life's stream unaided — you would be swept away by the current. It is therefore my earnest wish and desire that you should — with as little delay as may be decent — marry again; but be sure you select wisely, and choose for a husband some good fellow who will love you, and is a good honest fellow and a gentleman — like the bearer of this letter for instance. Do not fancy that you wrong my memory in doing this, my spirit will rejoice to see your happiness."

Brandon read this through slowly and looked at Mrs Sinclair.

The widow blushed, and cast down her eyes.

"Of course I must obey my husband's last wishes," she murmured — and the next moment she was in her lover's arms.

Doubt not, dear love, nor hesitate to say:
Blush if thou wilt; I love to see thy cheek
Grow hot with love-thoughts — let the word be said:
Between shy fingers whisper me the "yea"!
My soul will leap to hear as thine to speak.
Remember Love, forget the loveless bed;
Forget thy husband, and the cruel wreck
Of thy dear life on Wedlock's piteous sands:
Love's all in all, link on the golden bands
Forged in heaven without flaw or fleck.
I know thine answer by these amorous hands
That touch me thus to tempt me, by the kiss
Whose sudden passion burns upon my neck
Thy heart clings to me in a perfect "Yes!"

THE END

BIRCHGROVE PRESS
Flagellant & Libertine Erotica

Birchgrove Press specializes in producing new print and e-book editions of pre-1950s writings on sexual flagellation in English. Original editions of many of the books that we offer are difficult to obtain and are highly sought after. We are especially proud to offer new editions of rare Victorian flagellant texts such as *The Mysteries of Verbena House*, *Experimental Lecture by Colonel Spanker*, and *The Quintessence of Birch Discipline*. Birchgrove Press also produces new editions of libertine literature. We have published *Venus in the Cloister*, *The School of Venus*, *The Dialogues of Luisa Sigea*, and Isidore Liseux's translation of the Marquis de Sade's *Justine* (1791), *Opus Sadicum*, for example. For a full list of titles and formats, please visit our website:

www.birchgrovepress.com.